COMING FOR YOU

FOR YOU

But she is no victim

FRANCES MACKINTOSH

First edition independently published in the UK in 2023.
ISBN (Paperback):   978-1-7393619-0-7
Editor: Christine Beech
Typesetting & design: Matthew J Bird

A CIP catalogue record of this book is available from the British Library.

For further information about this book, please contact the author at:
francesmackintosh.author@gmail.com

For My Parents

Prologue

I'm dying.

This dusty stone tomb is completely dark and there are no shadows. Or maybe it's my eyes. They are so dry and itchy. I can no longer open them as my eyelids have stuck together. I've not drunk or eaten since being here.

Eleven days ago, the stone ground on which I lie felt so cold. So hard. Now I barely notice it. My body is shutting down. Fluid seeps from me. My underwear is wet. The only item of clothing my abductor has left me with.

Retribution.

I'm slowly choking on the thick substance in the back of my throat and my lungs are breaking down. I try to take a weak breath through cracked, painful lips. I'm drifting into my final sleep and my breathing is hindered. Very soon, death will take me.

Left deliberately to slowly die of unmitigated hunger.

I want my mother.

Chapter One
2004

I hear a gasp.

I pause for a split second before realising it has come from me.

I must get to work. I don't want to be late. I hate being late, it's rude. But I stop, without warning, and I can sense the frustration of others around me.

He's there again.

People are continuing to pass me by, maybe on their way to work or shopping. I don't care at this moment. He is staring intently at me from the other side of the road. His body is motionless, his stance confident.

This has been going on for about four months now. I don't know who he is. I can see him across the narrow road and he's always dressed the same, the man in the grey trench coat and trilby.

At first, I thought it was a coincidence. I seemed to keep bumping into him regularly. He has never approached or even tried to speak to me. He just stares, always watching. My mum always says there's no such thing as a coincidence.

I lower my head, denying myself the pleasure of the morning sun on my face. Hurrying towards the office, ignoring him, I wish I hadn't seen him. I can feel him watching me. I like to feel in control but this is making me anxious. An emotion I'm not familiar with.

Glancing at my watch, I quicken my pace. I'm five minutes away from my destination. It's 7.50 am and I start work at 8 am. I always wear heels. They look great but they slow me down. For the last five months, I've been getting the metro into the city centre, then it's twelve minutes to walk to work. It saves on driving in rush hour and expensive parking. I feel that the man watching me knows my weekly routine.

I can see the office block in front of me. It's a huge building with a glass front and a small café on the ground floor, used mainly for catchups with colleagues. The sun is reflecting off one of the huge windows. I love this time of year, late summer, with warm mornings and hours of daylight. The double doors open automatically and I take the stairs to the third floor where I work for an accountancy firm. P.E. Evans Accountancy, named after my boss. We are a small team of twenty-two and we all get on well. Unlike my last job, working with people who were over-promoted and without a clue. It's so true that you join an organisation but leave a manager. I work in finance as I prefer numbers to people.

I hurry along the white painted corridor. No pictures. It's very clinical. I stop when I reach the familiar solid wooden door with my name and job title on the small plaque, 'Faith Taylor – Personal Assistant.' I key in the door code C2468 which is easy to remember. My south-facing office is warm, so I slip off my navy jacket while stretching up to open a window. Throwing my Radley handbag under the desk with my other arm, I reach over to press the 'on' button and fire up the laptop. My desk is clear apart from the laptop, notebook and teacup. I hate clutter and I keep my private life very private. No naff family photos smile from my workspace.

I hear the adjoining door open and I know who it is without looking up. My boss is a man of routine. He wanders into my office with a small pile of papers in his hand. As a company, we are yet to go paperless.

"Good morning, Mr Evans."

"Morning, Faith. Can you deal with these, please?"

He hands me the papers. Some are letters and some are invoices. Not all our clients like to use email which frustrates me as it takes so much longer.

I smile at the middle-aged traditional man, now standing in my office space. Peter Evans is a good man and boss. I've been his secretary for three years. He's mild-mannered, a workaholic, and treats his team with respect. He always gets me a case of red for Christmas and discreetly overlooks the odd hangover I bring into the office after a night out with the girls or some guy I've been seeing that month. We have mutual respect. He's a traditionalist who dislikes me calling him by his first name. I've had other PA jobs in finance, for larger organisations, where it was common for the boss to sleep with one of the secretaries. Sex in the office before home time was a regular occurrence. Mr Evans is a loyal family man. I can't imagine him getting crumbs on his desk, never mind having reckless sex on it. I honestly don't think he would want to crease his suit.

As he turns to head back into his office, I turn my attention to the chrome kettle in the corner and flick the switch. It is one of my first jobs of the day; Mr Evan's white coffee, no sugar. My gaze wanders back to the window, watching the bright morning. Summer is nearly over and we are a few days away from September. The office overlooks the beginning of the city centre and, beyond that, a run-down housing estate.

He's there. The man with the grey trench coat.

Icy goosebumps stand to attention on my body and the back of my neck has gone cold as I involuntarily shiver. He's just standing there. On a public pavement, staring up at my office window. Is he looking at me? I might be paranoid, but my heart rate has increased and my hands feel clammy.

The figure in the grey trench coat continues to invade my life and, at night, my sleep. I've started to wake at night in fear. Sometimes my eyes snap open and I find myself upright, with no memory of when I sat up. My heart pounds, my mind is confused and the dreams are so vivid.

Always the same recurring dream. He's chasing me and there's no escape. I try to run but my legs won't work, or I dream I'm in a dark room and the lights won't work, and he's coming towards me in the grey trench coat, with his trilby hat pulled low on his face. I can't stop him. I'm in darkness. I'm trapped and each dream ends the same. He grabs my shoulders, we are face to face and I can't move.

I hate those dreams.

My mind has started to play tricks at night. I know I'm safe in the home I share with my parents, as I drift off to sleep in my room. But then I see him, near my bed. My hand frantically searches for the bedside lamp to cast his shadow and the terror away.

Knowing I'm safe in my office, I can't help staring back at him. He's motionless and just looking straight at me. He looks middle-aged, maybe older, lightly-built if not a little too skinny; it's hard to tell with the trench coat. His thinning grey hair is nearly shoulder-length and he has an unkempt look about him. My thoughts are racing. Do I know him? I don't think so. Is he undercover or an investigator? No, he stands out too much.

The kettle clicks off, drawing me sharply back to normality. Avoiding the hot steam, I make my flat white coffee.

Time passes quickly, it's been the usual busy day. Eight hours in front of the laptop, combined with the constant stream of incoming phone calls. I felt on edge most of the morning. Now I finally feel relief. Total relief. The man in the grey trench coat has disappeared and I can't see him anywhere out of the window. Sometimes I wonder if I should mention him to Mr Evans or even my parents, but I'm not one to worry people. I like to keep a low profile. I've never told a soul of my fear of the Grey Trench Coat Man.

Very soon I will deeply regret that decision. Later today, my life will change forever.

The best part of my day was another quick lunch with Aidan Handford, the new Debt Recovery Manager. The business does a lot of bookkeeping but not everyone wants to pay their bill. At thirty-five years old, he's seven years older than me. He's your stereotypical tall, dark and handsome guy. Rumour has it that he's a player and I plan to find out. The physical attraction between us was instant when we first met three months ago, but neither of us have mentioned it. Instead, we flirt and make small talk. He's Mr Evan's deputy, so seeing him regularly is easy and part of my job.

I don't know if he's married. I don't care. I have no plans to marry him. Just borrow him. He doesn't wear a wedding ring but that doesn't mean anything. He never talks about his private life and doesn't do social media. I've checked.

As time was tight and we both had a load of work to do, we went to the small café near the office block. He looked very attractive in his blue suit and what I could only describe as a blush shirt; a pale pink. He wore brown shoes, thankfully with socks. I know the trend today is for men not to wear socks but it looks like they've left the house in a hurry.

The Pure Apple Café only has five tables as most of its trade is takeout. It only does a vegan menu. I like a plant-based diet at times but I love a bacon sandwich more. Aidan, on the other hand, is vegan and hasn't eaten meat for ten years. Since I wanted to see more of him, I ordered a roasted butternut squash and black bean salad for lunch washed down with a cup of green tea known as Matcha. The salad and Matcha were both very good.

"Would you like to go for dinner on Saturday night?"

Aidan was looking directly at me for a reaction. I felt a surge of excitement and casually replied, "Okay, sure."

"Good, I'll pick you up at 7.30 pm then. Can you text me your address?"

Nodding and trying to play it cool, I casually responded, keeping the excitement out of my voice, "Looking forward to it. Shall we head back?"

Suppressing emotion usually comes easy to me and it comes in handy when you've just been asked out by someone you like. Together we left the café and walked briskly back, in contented silence.

*

My mind wanders as I think about what to wear for our first date tomorrow, and he is probably thinking about which restaurant will impress me the most. I hope there is chicken on the menu.

It's now five o'clock. Home time and that great feeling of no work for two days. I never tire of that feeling. Freedom and lie-ins for two whole days. I log off, knowing the start of my weekend is only minutes away.

I collect my things, close the window, and pop my head through the adjourning door. Mr Evans glances up from his desk.

"Have a good weekend. Doing anything special?"

He's smiling at me.

"No, nothing planned apart from a meal."

I keep the excitement out of my voice.

"See you Monday then."

"Yes, here's the mail for your signature."

I hand him a blue cardboard file.

At that moment, I did not know I would never return.

Chapter Two

Outside the comfort and safety of the office block, I look around intensively. There is no sign of him. No sign of the Grey Trench Coat Man. Yet again, I experience relief sweep through me as I head determinedly towards the metro station, my thoughts drifting to Aidan. It is still very warm; I'm not sure how much is to do with the time of year, August, or global warming. Either way, it lifts my mood. I feel content and happy.

At twenty-eight years of age, I've never had a serious relationship. I like my freedom. Most of my relationships have lasted six months or less, and my parents joke if I'll ever leave home. I'm not planning on it. I save most of my wages each month and I don't have to cook, do laundry or clean. My mum, Martha, is fifty-eight years young and still attractive but plump; not that I'd ever say that to her. She's also easy-going and very talkative, takes pride in her family and runs a loving home. Her husband, James, my father, is quiet, reserved and likes to keep an eye on the finances, unlike Mum who likes to spend. At sixty-two, Mum is never going to change Father's ways. I was three months old when they adopted me and took me into their very warm hearts and home. They are the only parents I have ever known.

My birth mother didn't know who my birth father was, and she died about ten years ago in one of Her Majesty's prisons. I think it may have been HMP Durham. No one speaks about her. I never knew her and never want to. She was incarcerated

14

for stabbing her then-boyfriend and, as he lay dying, she poured a bottle of bleach over his head to finish him off. It wasn't her first offence.

I feel the darkness within me that must have run through her veins too, to kill and destroy the guy so easily. So far, I have suppressed it. It's my dark secret. My birth mother died in prison from a drug overdose. I was eighteen years old when my mother told me, but I felt no emotion. She was a stranger to me.

I picture what it must feel like to kill someone. To be responsible for taking their life. If I took someone's life, would I feel guilty or powerful? I read that psychopaths don't feel guilt or empathy and they usually dislike or torture animals. Whilst I fantasise about murder, according to the experts I'm no psychopath. I love animals and I even have a cat. She's jet-black and called Snowy. I also have a sense of humour. I love my cat and I'd never harm her.

I continue towards the metro station, thinking about what to wear for the date. Should I go for a sexy look? Or a classy one? I could combine the two. I'm picturing a pair of jeans, a black off-the-shoulder top and sandals, with my blonde hair tousled.

Someone has grabbed my arm.

Shocked, I stop. My brain tries to process what has just happened. An elderly lady with thin, pale twisted fingers is gripping my arm and gasping for breath.

"Help me," she said, her voice no more than a whisper.

Still feeling stunned, I lean in to hear her as I ask, "What's wrong?"

She smells of mould and dampness. It's unpleasant and my nose twitches, trying to block the smell of stale body odour combined with pee. She points with her free arm to her chest and her breathing is heavy and slow.

"Chest pains. My heart isn't what it used to be."

The woman doesn't look well. Stick-thin, she looks in her late seventies, is shabby in appearance and her thin arthritic fingers are still clutching my arm. Her white hair is short and very fine and, although you can see her scalp in places, there's a natural wave to it. The shock is starting to leave me. I need to focus. She's old and I've got a metro to catch but there's no one else in sight. Damn it!

"I'll call you an ambulance," I say, as I start to rummage in my large navy Radley bag in search of my mobile phone; remembering that I still need to text Aidan my address.

"No, no need. Would you see me home? I live just five minutes from here and I've got medication there. I'm not dying in a bleeding hospital. Rather go in my own bed."

She is pointing in the direction of the run-down housing estate. I've seen it before from my office window. Many of the properties are empty and boarded-up. It would cost less to demolish the estate than to return the properties to a habitable state.

My heart sinks. I'm going to miss the 5.20 pm metro but thankfully they run every eleven minutes.

Still wheezing, the old woman points towards Bowman Street, the street I had just passed when my thoughts were filled with sunshine and Aidan Handford. My instincts are screaming at me. I feel on edge as if something isn't right. I'm looking at her. She needs help and there's no one else around. I must help her, yet I feel anxious and irritated by the delay. She still smells funny, slightly musty. Up close she looks about ten years younger, she could be early sixties. It's hard to tell.

I take the shopping bag hanging from her arm. It's very light but smells the same as its owner. I'm going to need a shower when I finally get home.

With a sigh, I turn back the way I came and slowly we make our way along the street. The old woman is clinging to me as if her remaining time depends on it. I don't know her name. I stop myself from asking as I just want to see her home and catch the metro. I hope I don't smell like her.

We continue to walk in silence. I still feel on edge and frustrated that I'll be getting home late. My tea will be ready. My mum is a great cook. I wish I was at home.

The street is deserted. Most people, unless they live here, avoid this area. It has a feeling of hopelessness about it. We turn left down another street. It certainly isn't the best area in town. The North of England is often depicted in the media as a dump. It doesn't help that, when covering local stories, journalists often choose people who can't string a sentence together. This part of town lives up to its reputation of deprivation. Until the suits in local government decide what to do with it, some houses stand abandoned. I thought there was a housing crisis. There must be about sixteen houses in this street all boarded-up, apart from three. I presume they are privately owned but I doubt the owners would ever be able to sell them. This is a different world from where my parents live; detached houses with gardens and a feeling of success. Neighbours out on Sundays, either washing their already-clean cars or doing their immaculate gardens.

"That's it there."

She's pointing to one of the three houses. It looks how she smells. Decaying. The garden is wild and overgrown.

Yellowed net curtains hang in the downstairs windows and one window upstairs is boarded-up. I have replaced annoyance with pity. I feel sorry for this old woman and how she seems forgotten by society and is immersed in a life of poverty. I smile at her and decide I'm going to give her the £20 note I have in my purse. Hopefully, she'll be able to get some food and shower gel.

Removing a key from her coat pocket, I help her into the house; the now-familiar smell of dampness continues to invade my nostrils. She moves around me to close the front door and locks it. Maybe her age makes her safety-conscious. My heart is racing and my head is telling me to run. Now. Get out. My instincts are never wrong.

"I have to get home. Are you okay if I leave you now?" I ask, helping her into the front room and a chair. "Do you feel any better? Where's your medication?"

She's looking straight at me and there's a coldness in her eyes I haven't noticed before. She looks a lot better, a lot younger even, now that she is seated in her own home. She's smiling at me but it's an icy smile. I want to get out. I don't know why. She's old. I'm fit and work out regularly. I can easily overpower her.

"I must be going now. Is there anyone you want me to call?"

Her eyes are set on me. Small, uncaring eyes. Eyes that say something is about to happen. Goosebumps cover my arms and the back of my neck.

"Stay for a cup of tea," she says as she begins to rise from her grubby chair. "To thank you. You are the only visitor we've had in a year."

"Who's we?" I ask.

She ignores my question and steadily makes her way into what I presume is the kitchen. I don't know what to do. I want to run. She looks harmless and I feel sorry for her. No one should be living here. I watch as she heads to the kitchen. Her face is savaged by old age and poor living, some of her teeth are missing and a blue polyester dress hangs from her skeletal frame. She looks malnourished. I'll take note of her address and ring Social Services on Monday.

As I wait for her to make the tea I don't want, I take in my surroundings. The front room is dark, partly because of the grime on the windows blocking out the light of the watery sun. The furniture looks to be from the 1970s. Cobwebs hang from the ceiling, yellowed newspapers are scattered in piles and there's mail lying on a small table, unopened. I resist the urge to scratch. This room is a breeding ground for fleas, insects and vermin. The smell of urine is overwhelming. Years of filth, grime and neglect surround me, yet she seems to not notice.

She's back, with two cracked mugs of tea. At one time, they were plain white. I take a sip. It's very hot but I'm eager to finish it so I can leave. It tastes slightly odd. The milk is probably on the turn.

She's seated again, opposite me, observing me. I feel I'm about to be condemned.

"What's your name?"

"It's Faith."

She laughs. I like my name. I don't know why she finds it amusing.

"Oh, the irony," she says, still laughing.

My mood has changed from pity to annoyance and I find her rude and ungrateful. I should have ignored her when she

19

asked for my help. Kept on walking and left her for someone else to help.

"Are you feeling any better?" I ask, out of politeness as I ignore her last remark. My instinct still urges me to get out of her house. Now.

"Better. I'm excited and relieved it's over."

She's laughing again. She's getting on my nerves and I'm puzzled by her response. Before I can question what she means, I hear the front door open and slam shut.

"Is that you, Son?"

She is now beaming. No longer the sick, vulnerable person.

I will not be going home or out to dinner with Aidan tomorrow night. Fear has paralysed me and I can't move. The man in the grey trench coat enters the room with a chilling sneer on his face.

"You have done well, Mother," he says as he moves towards me.

Chapter Three

The wind was angry, the sky slate-grey. It was typical for a Monday morning; awful weather for August. The ladies held on to their black hats, the gentlemen pulled the collars of their black overcoats high. The rain teemed down but no one standing at the freshly-dug graveside in St Paul's Cemetery seemed to notice. United in grief, they shared feelings of despair and misery at the loss of such a young life.

Her end had been long and painful, and she had suffered greatly. This fact was etched on the congregation's minds as they stood around the open grave with a pool of water starting to settle at the bottom. Her coffin, carrying one red rose, waited to be lowered into the damp earth. Aunt Dorothy dabbed at her eyes, thinking how wet and cold her niece was going to be, buried on such a dismal day. Not that it mattered as her soul was free and had gone on to better things.

Aidan Handford felt torn. He hadn't known the deceased very well, but well enough. His gaze remained downwards as he stared at his highly-polished black shoes.

People always stare down at their shoes at funerals. Better than staring at faces of grief.

The Reverend Simon Graham was addressing the congregation but Aunt Dorothy, a widow, was not listening. Her thoughts were cast back to her deceased niece's childhood.

She had such a happy childhood.

Dorothy had raised her niece single-handedly. She could still picture her in her school uniform on her first day at Infants, then Juniors, followed by Senior School.

How time flies.

She could remember the tantrums because she would never let her stay out after 10 pm, even when she had reached sixteen. Then there was her first boyfriend, Peter, who now stood at the graveside, his face expressionless.

Aunt Dorothy was a proud, plump, smart lady, although you could not consider her working life to be a career. She had worked hard and supported herself and her niece adequately. Always cooking for her from scratch. 'Eating clean' they call it today. Normal life and not being lazy was how Aunt Dorothy saw it. Her niece had loved her pies, casseroles and cakes. Everything was homemade as she didn't like the idea of eating processed food or 'muck'.

The house was always warm, clean and tidy. The door was always open to those who needed a shoulder to cry on. The opposite of Aunt Dorothy's childhood, or Dot to her friends. She kept her memories tightly locked in her mind until she moved in with her grandparents. Her birth parents had no time for their three children as they were too wrapped up in each other. Dot was the friend everyone wanted and needed, everyone who met her, liked her. Apart from her older sister, Elizabeth. They had not spoken in years and Elizabeth accused Dorothy of abandoning her. She had wanted to live with their grandparents too but they had found young Elizabeth unsociable and withdrawn.

Elizabeth had nothing to do with her family. Today was no exception, she hadn't made an appearance.

Dot's thoughts ended abruptly because of the commotion around her. The deceased's birth mother had turned up. Natalie Winter, Dot's younger sister. It had been decades since any of the family had seen Natalie or Elizabeth. The sight was pitiful. Natalie was lying on top of the white coffin, clinging to it, awash with drink, guilt and grief.

Natalie looked older than her early-fifties. Her appearance didn't fit with the smartly-dressed, sombre crowd. She was in black leggings, worn boots and an off-white parka. Her hair was wet from the heavy rain and her face showed the story of a hard wasted life.

"Why?" she sobbed.

Dot stood motionless, taking in the nauseating scene before her. Surely it should be her who was overcome with grief? A middle-aged man from the congregation stepped forward, followed by another mourner. After a short scuffle involving Natalie trying to kick both of them, they removed the deceased's birth mother from the white coffin. She was ushered quickly towards a member of the cemetery staff who must have come from the small church nearby. The single red rose from Aunt Dorothy lay crushed on the earth.

The Reverend Graham quickly wrapped up the short service. The congregation stood in silence as the coffin was lowered into the ground. A small white cross marked the spot until her headstone would be ready. It read 'Abbey Jessica Winter 10 November 1974 - 06 August 2004.' She was only twenty-nine. Aidan Handford's second cousin.

Abbey had been one of those people who would light up a room and whose beauty matched her personality. Dot had taught her to treat others as she expected to be treated herself, to have goals in life and follow her heart. She would be greatly

23

missed. She had been the love of Dot's life, who thanked the Lord that she was with Abbey in her final hours before she faded away. The cancer had finally taken her.

Thirty minutes later, the soaked congregation had gathered at Dot's house for sherry and a buffet. All homemade and all Abbey's favourite things. The atmosphere had lightened a little, probably thanks to the sherry, and most of the guests were reminiscing about Abbey. Dot wished they would all hurry up and leave so that she could get on with the washing up and get the house back to the way Abbey liked it. Spick and span.

At 3 pm the guests finally started to leave. Aidan offered to stay and help clear up, but she was having none of it. Instead, he hugged her at the doorway and briskly strode to his car. The day had turned chilly but at least the rain had stopped.

Once inside the car, away from the hustle and bustle, his thoughts returned to Faith. He wondered why she hadn't been in touch to arrange their night out. He envisaged her blonde hair, slim figure and long legs and heaved a long sigh of regret.

I'll ask her out again next week. Offer to cook her supper. Women often like that sort of thing.

Faith wouldn't be there for supper. She was living a nightmare.

Chapter Four

I'm in shock. My brain is struggling to comprehend what is happening. I am unable to move. My body has frozen. I can see my fingers tight around the mug of tea, and my knuckles are white. I can taste something strange in my throat, it's fear. Moving only my eyes, I'm looking directly at the old woman. Her face holds a gleeful look. You could describe it as a smirk.

My brain seems to have engaged. I know I'm in danger. Real danger. The man who has followed me is only feet away and I'm trapped. My instincts are screaming out to run but I can't move. My body has shut down and I can't get out of the chair.

"She's very pretty, William," says the old woman, with a grin. "She'll make a perfect mother for your first child."

"Perfect, isn't she? And she's finally here. In our home, after all this time. Now she's part of our family," chuckles William.

They are both laughing as if this is a normal situation. Stalking and entrapment. I find my voice.

"You're sick. Both of you. Insane."

I'm terrified and enraged. Fear that paralysed me seconds ago has switched to burning anger. I will survive this. They don't know the darkness I secretly carry within. The fantasies I have had to control. A slight flicker of excitement flashes through me. I might get to try some of them out. This is the perfect situation. Self-defence. I'm leaving.

I push myself out of the chair, throwing the cup and some of the tea violently towards the old woman, aiming for her smug face. I don't know if it has hit her. My eyes close and I have an overpowering need to vomit. I feel faint and my sight is going. I'm losing consciousness. I can only see darkness.

I collapse over the chair and my face takes the impact of the fall. I should have known better. The old cow has drugged the tea.

*

My face hurts. I can feel my heart palpitating. I'm conscious but I don't want to open my eyes as I'm afraid of what they'll see. I remember vaguely what happened. I remember that I was going to faint. I've no idea how long I've been unconscious. I brace myself and slowly open my eyes.

Nothing is familiar. I'm in new surroundings.

Time has yellowed the ceiling and there's a naked light bulb above my head. I'm confused. My brain doesn't recognise what my eyes see. I push myself up into a sitting position. The smell of dampness is invading my nostrils.

I'm in a room, on a bed. The wallpaper has a large floral pattern, hideous orange and brown. It's hanging off in strips where the wall is too damp to hold it up. To my left, there's a battered dark wooden bedside cabinet with nothing on top of it. No alarm clock, book or bedside lamp.

The bed I'm sitting on stinks of pee. There's one blanket that is threadbare, as is the folded purple bedspread at the bottom of the bed. There are black circles, in various sizes over it, which look like mould.

I've just had a sickening thought. I hope this isn't his room. The Grey Trench Coat Man, or William, as his mother called him. I need to get out. I am so thirsty and my mouth is so dry.

I stumble off the bed. My head is throbbing as I have an almighty headache. Looking down, I experience some relief. I'm fully-dressed and they haven't tied my hands.

I feel strangely calm and sleepy as if this isn't happening to me. Walking towards the only small window in the room, I can't see the view outside. A film of grime and dirt, built up over the years, obscures it. As for the bars, they are solid. Something tells me I am not the first person to end up here. They've done this before.

Why me? I push the thought quickly from my head and try the door. As expected, it's locked but there is no keyhole so it must be bolted from the outside. I wander around my new surroundings; they are so dirty and neglected. I can't think straight. My legs are heavy and walking is such an effort. Tiredness is taking over. I can't fight it, it's so strong. I need to lie down. The bed stinks but it's better than the floor. I know I'm drifting back again into a drugged sleep.

*

I don't know how long I've slept or how long I've been here. Have I woken up? Am I dreaming or is the sensation I'm experiencing real? I feel disorientated. Is someone brushing my hair?

"Hello, Dear. Sleep well?"

The Grey Trench Coat Man is here. He's in my space, smiling at me. My vision feels weird. Slightly out of focus.

I spring upright, still on the bed. Or I try to. My reflexes are slow.

"What! What are you doing?"

I'm so confused. I push his scrawny hand away. How has this happened to me? What day is it? And my parents? Oh God, what are they doing now? Do they realise I'm missing?

*

The smile fell from thirty-four-year-old William Channing's emaciated face. He looked much older than his years. His long wispy hair, which his mother cuts, didn't help. He was confused.

Mother said she would love me. Why, then, is she mad at me? Doesn't she know all I want to do is take care of her? I came into her room to check on her and noticed that her hair needed brushing.

Getting up from the bed, he left the room, slamming the door behind him.

*

I need to focus. I need to get out of this creepy house. I look around the small, damp room for my bag. Damn it. It must still be downstairs, along with my mobile phone.

The door opens. He's here again. This time, with a bucket.

"Go away. Leave me alone!"

"Your supper is ready. You have to get washed."

He is softly spoken with a northern intonation and there's an expectant look in his green eyes.

I'm struggling for words as none of this seems real. I am just about to object when he thrusts a soapy sponge in my face. He's rough and is washing my face like a child who has devoured ice cream.

"There, you're all nice and clean."

He smiles, happy with his work.

I feel physically sick as he tries to dry my face with a towel. It stinks. I slap his arm away. It smells the same as this room. Rotten. I'm staring at him in disbelief as I can't believe what has just happened. Being washed as if I'm a toddler. Except there were no loving gentle movements in his hands. They were rough and frenzied as if the experience had excited him.

I watch him leave the room but he's back after only a few seconds, carrying a round tray. Something on it smells faintly familiar. Nausea washes over me again. I don't want to eat. I want water.

"Here you go. Supper. You like fish, don't you? I've seen you buy it in the supermarket."

I have nothing to say. I'm taking in his thin frame and the bony hands clasped around the tray. He must have been following me around without me knowing. I can't remember the last time I bought fish. My mind can't focus. I rarely go food shopping. There's no need as my tea is usually ready when I get in. My mum takes care of it.

I need to win William round. It has worked for me so far in my life. Adapting my behaviour to fit in.

"Thank you."

I take the tray slowly from him. I'm not hungry but I remember reading a story about a soldier who had been captured and survived in the Middle East. His training had kicked in and he played a subservient role, so as not to antagonise his capturer. Here it goes. Submission time.

"What do you want with me, and when do you think I can go home?"

I stare straight into his aroused eyes as I ask the questions. I'm searching his face for the answers I need.

He looks baffled.

"But you are home. I'm going to look after you, feed you, clothe you and wash you. You are meant to be with me. I've been watching you for a long time. You've been watching me from your office window. You're so different to the rest."

I don't reply. I don't know anything about stalkers. Do they often kill their victims? He doesn't look strong enough to kill me.

He's leaving the room again. This time I hear a bolt being locked from the other side. I've no idea how long I've been here. I hope my parents have called the police and they track my mobile phone.

My stomach growls with hunger so I decide to take a chance and taste the fish. I'm surprised as it tastes fine. There's a slight flavour of milk and butter, three boiled potatoes and a small serving of carrots on the chipped plate. I'm so thirsty that I can hardly swallow. There's no water on the tray but there's a mug of tea. The mug looks familiar. Surely they haven't drugged this one? I'm wary. It smells fine. Taking a small sip, it tastes slightly bitter and it's hot. Thirst takes over and I gulp it down, burning my tongue.

I wish I hadn't given in to the thirst. Given in to his plan. With time, comes the familiar sensation of losing consciousness. My senses fail and I know darkness is about to follow. My body twitches from the effects I will later find out are Ketamine and Amtyl. Sleeping pills.

*

I wake to what I presume is the next day as daylight fills the room, which makes it look even more run-down than I remember. Do people really live in so much filth? I feel strangely chilled out. I know I was dreaming but I can't remember clearly what it was about. I just remember the feeling of helplessness. My heart is racing and I want a bath. My body feels detached as if I'm not in control of its movements. I huddle the worn blanket around me. I no longer notice the smell of dampness and urine. I have become habituated.

I only have my underwear on! Where's my dress? What has he done to me? There are no memories. I can't remember taking it off. I can't remember him taking it off either. Panic rises within me but I don't have the strength to move. I'm so tired. I feel helpless. I don't do helpless. I have a darkness within me. I am no victim.

"WILLIAM, WILLIAM!"

Anger erupts inside me. I've had enough. Having no control over the situation has suddenly fired my ugly temper. An uncontrollable rage. I want to kill him. I want to feel the pleasure of watching him die. My body feels strange. I feel disconnected from it as I find myself at the door, pounding it with clenched fists.

"LET ME OUT, NOW, WILLIAM. I'LL KILL YOU AND YOUR BITCH OF A MOTHER."

I've lost control as adrenaline surges through me. The door opens abruptly. I don't attack as this isn't what I was expecting. What I see is sickening.

"What's all the noise for, you naughty girl?"

I recognise the voice but his appearance has changed.

I find my legs carrying me backwards to the safety of the pee-stained bed. William is wearing my blue polka-dot dress but it's open at the back. A blonde wig, in an identical style to my natural long hair. His face is masked in badly-applied makeup. Even his lipstick is the shade I usually wear. He has a familiar smell about him. I remember that Red Petal scent. He's wearing my favourite perfume.

I can't step back any further as my legs are up against the bed. Blind fury has turned to confusion and panic. I don't know what this means.

"Why are you afraid? Why are you afraid of yourself?"

Before I can respond, William continues.

"You see, Faith. I love you. I am you. I want to be you. I want us to be one person."

Slowly lifting my arms to waist height, I take the breakfast tray which he's carrying. We are staring at each other. He's about four inches taller than my 5ft 7in frame and his skinny legs are sticking out from under my dress. Without thinking, I hurl the tray and its contents with all my strength. It strikes him hard against his left shoulder and hot tea burns his left arm. For a second, he doesn't move as the toast and an empty cup lie at his feet. He doesn't seem to notice the pain. He is confused by my anger. His left hand smacks my right cheek. I feel little pain but the impact knocks me onto the bed. I freeze as I watch him, fearful of what will happen next.

It isn't what I expect. I expect him to attack me. Instead, he slowly turns away from me and heads out of the room, pausing momentarily to turn his head and look at me, with his lips partly open as if to speak. Whatever he was about to say he keeps to himself and a smile crosses his thin lips.

*

You are not going anywhere. Not until you give me a child. There have been seventeen others before you and none of them left here alive.

Chapter Five

Aidan stood in the shower, the jet of cool water invigorating both mind and body. He felt mentally drained after such a long, disheartening day. Stepping from the shower, he rough-dried his dark hair and then wrapped a towel around his waist as he wandered into his bedroom.

In front of the mirror, he admired his physique. His skin was tanned, his dark brown hair cut short. He stood tall, even in bare feet, and his body was toned from working out regularly at the gym. He stepped closer to the mirror to examine his face. It was clean-shaven with blue eyes, a Roman nose and white teeth. He studied his eyes again. There were a few deep lines around them which he told himself were laughter lines. They gave his face character. The reflection pleased him.

Faith entered his thoughts once more. Her slim figure, blonde hair, green eyes and the desire he felt for her.

Play it cool.

He had played it too cool. She hadn't even bothered to turn up. He wasn't used to being stood up. He smiled again at the thought. She just needed more persuading and he loved a challenge.

He always wanted sex. Any woman who took care of themselves would do. Never married, he was proud of his bachelor status at thirty-five. He had his own house, car and money in the bank. What more did a man want? Material items meant more to him than a solid, reliable relationship. He thought the opposite sex would find him less attractive if he was married. He had never been faithful in any of his relationships. They all eventually failed so what was the point of missing any fun that came his way? His exes called him vain, selfish and self-centred. He, in return, gave them a good time and bought them expensive gifts. He couldn't see their problem.

He picked up the telephone next to his bed and dialled a number that he knew well. The telephone rang twice before a female voice answered.

"Hello."

"Hi, Babe. Just thought I'd invite you to supper."

"Aidan? It's 9 o'clock. I was going to have an early night."

"Oh, come on, Imogen. I'll order pizza," persuaded Aidan.

Silence.

"See you in half an hour. You got any Beaujolais?" asked Imogen.

Aidan replaced the receiver, pleased with himself as he lay back on his bed.

Imogen will do for this evening.

Their friendship had started about seven years ago when they met in Figures Nightclub near the coast. She had been with a group of friends but she had stood out. Brunette, tall, slim; just the way he liked them. She was wearing a short red dress but she had style and class.

That night had been the beginning of their friendship. They were more like friends than lovers but they had an understanding. If they bumped into each other at the end of a night out they would go home together, and sometimes they would even go shopping for their groceries together. Aidan loved Imogen as a friend. Imogen was in love with Aidan but was smart enough to know that, if she ever told him, she would lose him. He didn't want commitment; he wanted the best of both worlds. She stood by him and forgave whatever he did. She was always there for him, waiting in the background. She thought of the saying, 'Everything comes to those who wait.' She'd certainly done that.

The doorbell rang and Aidan jumped up from the bed to answer it, putting all thoughts of Faith out of his mind. There stood Imogen, looking as seductive as ever. He grabbed her arm and led her to the bedroom where they stayed until morning. The pizza was never ordered, and the wine never corked.

In the morning, Imogen let herself out. She was famished as they hadn't stopped to eat last night. She smiled at the memory while glancing at her watch. There was just enough time to nip home, grab a bite to eat, shower, and then rush to the office.

*

Imogen Fernsby worked for the local newspaper. She was a crime reporter but her job frustrated her. Week in, week out, her reports were very similar; cars stolen daily, homes broken into, old people attacked in daylight, young kids stabbed and no justice for the guilty. The world was an ugly place in Imogen's eyes. What she really liked to do was write fiction, especially children's books, where her mind could wander into a fantasy world with talking animals, clear blue skies and happy people. Being an author was on her bucket list.

When she arrived at work, half an hour later than usual, there were half a dozen messages on her desk and she started to wade through them while waiting for the kettle to boil. One message stood out from the rest. A young woman had disappeared on her way home on the previous Friday night. Vanished into thin air. Could she go and interview the girl's parents and run a missing story? She'd call her contact at the Police Press Office.

The scribbled message on her desk from her colleague said they had very little to work on. Imogen read on.

A 28-year-old white woman had left her office at the end of the working day as usual but never made it home. Her friends hadn't heard from her and she didn't have a regular boyfriend.

Typical. It had to be a Friday night after work when no one notices anything as they are too preoccupied with getting home for the start of the weekend.

There was no signal from the missing girl's mobile phone and her bank cards hadn't been used. CCTV from her office building showed her leaving the office where she worked but there was no sign of her catching her usual metro on the train station's CCTV.

Imogen drank her coffee and picked up her mobile phone. She glanced at the photo of the missing girl again, checked out the address of the parents and left her office for the start of another day.

The weather was mild and the trees swayed slightly in the breeze, but it was a big improvement on the recent weather of strong winds and heavy showers. It hadn't felt like summer lately.

Twenty-five minutes later, Imogen pulled up near a smart semi-detached house. She quickly checked her appearance in the car mirror before heading up the short drive to ring the doorbell. The door was answered quickly by a lady in her late fifties who was very smart but had a look of bewilderment in her eyes.

"Good morning. I'm Imogen Fernsby from News Today," said Imogen as she extended her hand to Mrs Taylor.

"We were expecting you. Please come in. I'm Martha."

Once inside, Martha Taylor introduced the journalist to her husband, James Taylor. Imogen immediately noticed that, despite their anguish, they were close to each other and even looked similar.

Probably been happily married for years.

A black cat jumped onto Martha's lap. It did an elegant circle then settled down, purring contentedly.

"This is Snowy, Faith's cat," smiled Martha, as she slowly stroked its velvety back. Imogen nodded knowingly. She loved animals too.

Seated next to an anxious James was a young woman. She looked a little like the photo Imogen had already seen of Faith. The same long blonde hair and a similar style of clothes.

"This is Rebecca, Faith's best friend," James explained.

"Hello. I'm Imogen Fernsby," she said, extending her hand.

"Rebecca Bixby."

Imogen thought that Rebecca was about to burst into tears. The two girls must have been close.

"I know this is hard for you," she began, "but I need to ask a few questions and, hopefully when we run the story, someone might remember seeing Faith on her way home."

Unfortunately, the parents had very little to tell. The morning of Faith's disappearance had been no different to any other. There had been no strange phone calls, she had left the house at the same time, and they had searched her bedroom for clues but there were none. They just didn't understand it as all her clothes were still there, apart from the blue polka dot dress she wore to work that morning. Faith was so happy at home; why would she want to leave? They had searched for an answer but they didn't have one.

They had rung her mobile phone on Friday but it had gone straight to voicemail. The police had tried to pick up a signal but there wasn't one. The last time she'd used her phone was at work when she'd sent a text to Rebecca about a date she was going on that weekend. Imogen noted that she worked at the same place as Aidan but Rebecca didn't know who Faith's date had been.

As Imogen left the Taylors' house with a more recent photo of Faith, she promised to keep in touch. She didn't feel the story would lead to much. She expected the girl had gone off with some guy. Deciding against going back to the office, she thought she would call in on Aidan and have lunch with him. She smiled to herself. He'd taken today off and would probably still be in bed. She might join him.

She was right. When Aidan finally answered the door, he was bleary-eyed and only wearing a robe.

"You should get some sleep at night," she teased.

Smiling, he stood back to let her in.

"Thought I would take you to lunch," she said. She playfully poked him in the stomach as she walked past, heading to the kitchen.

"Great idea. I'll jump in the shower and, in the meantime, you can put the kettle on."

He kissed the top of her head before leaving her to make them some coffee. She knew where everything was. Removing the coffee jar from a cupboard with one hand, she started to read her notes on the missing girl. The enclosed photo showed her smiling.

You are very attractive. I wonder where you are, or if you are still alive.

She had made a mental note, after speaking to the parents, to ask Aidan after Martha had informed her that Faith worked at P.E. Evans Accountancy. The same place as Aidan.

As he wandered back into the kitchen, dressed and showered, he saw her deep in thought.

"Something interesting?"

"A missing person's case but unfortunately not much to go on," answered Imogen. "Very attractive though, yet no one saw her on her way home."

Idly, she handed him the passport-size photo Rebecca had given her.

"Apparently she works at your place."

He didn't realise he was holding his breath. He felt a pang of guilt for shrugging off so easily the fact she hadn't sent him a text to arrange their date. Noticing a change in her on-off lover, Imogen guessed what he was about to say, so she asked, "Do you know her?"

"Yes, she works at my place. You won't like this, but I was supposed to meet her on Saturday night but she didn't text to make any arrangements," he confessed.

Imogen looked at Aidan and then slowly back at the photo. She wasn't sure if she wanted Faith to be found.

Chapter Six

I'm wandering around the cold bare dirty room, finding it hard to think straight. I'm not sure how many days I've been captured now. Is it three or four? Why hasn't anyone come for me? I'd love a bath. I much prefer baths to showers, but I'm not asking William. The lunatic would probably be happy to bathe me like a baby. He still has my dress and I still only have my underwear on. I'll never wear my dress again now that he has touched it, even in this cold.

The house is so quiet, I haven't seen or heard his mother since I've been here. I hope she's died some horrible death, but I doubt it. She's probably out shopping somewhere or picking up other prey. Since refusing to drink any more tea, I can think slightly better. I picture what I will do to his mother when I finally get out of here. I picture taking my revenge slowly while he watches.

I need to find a way out but the bars at the window are solid. I can reach the glass behind them but I don't know what's on the other side. Maybe I'm in the front bedroom, which means the overgrown garden will be below me. There seems little point in breaking the glass as there are no neighbours. I would probably just end up with an icy blast filling the room. I'm shivering with the cold and have no choice but to wrap the dirty blanket around me. It stinks. I stink.

Damn it, I've had enough.

"WILLIAM, WILLIAM!"

"What is it, Dear?"

The door swings open and he's there, still looking ridiculous in my dress. There's a weird stain on the front but I don't want to know what it is.

"I want to go home. I'm sick of your games. You don't know me, you don't know anything about me."

My temper is rising.

He looks serious, turns and leaves the room. I hear the bolt slide across. The sound is becoming very familiar. Moments later, I hear the bolt again and he has returned. He's carrying a battered red book and what looks like a photo album. I can already sense I'm not going to like what is about to happen.

"Come, sit beside me," gestures William, his voice soft.

He is seated on the bed and seems oblivious to the smell and the dampness. I hesitate. He has closed the door but I know it's not locked. It only locks from the outside. Shall I make a run for it?

"Sit."

His tone is firm.

Slowly, I move a little nearer, curiosity taking over. Stretching my neck, I look at the red book in his pale bony hands. I sit on the opposite end of the bed. My eyes glance at the closed door.

"Today," he reads, "Faith was wearing a black skirt and red jacket. She had one hour for lunch and went shopping for some makeup. She also bought a sandwich. When she left the office at 5.30 pm she looked a little tired, but content. I followed her to make sure she got home safely."

I feel sick. He knows my name and where I live. I'd never noticed him following me home. My parents! Are they safe?

"You see, I do know you, Faith. I've been writing about your life for months."

I say nothing. I don't know what to say. I can see his handwriting is childlike and littered with spelling errors. I'm not sure if he can read or write properly. He opens the box which contains photos of me printed on A4 paper. How had I not noticed him all this time? I'd seen him when he wanted to be seen. This is worse than I had imagined. No one seems to know I'm here. I could be missing for years. My mind snaps back to William's reading.

"Faith met someone for lunch today. They seemed very happy. They were laughing and talking the whole time. I am not happy about this. I need to speak to Mother. She will know what to do."

He continues to read out loud but I have switched off. His words stick in my mind. It now makes sense. He had his mother capture me because he had seen me with Aidan and was jealous.

He has studied my life, my ways and my routine. It explains how he knows which perfume I wear, which brand of makeup I use and how he used to turn up unexpectedly. He is totally obsessed and very dangerous.

"That was my brother you saw me with. He took me for lunch. He will be worried about me. You have to let me go."

I'm pleading with him.

"Don't lie, you don't have a brother. If I can't have you, no one will, not even Aidan. See, I even know his name. I told you I know everything about you."

Calmly, he rises from the bed and, pausing at the door, continues, "He's also sleeping with other women. He doesn't deserve you."

I'm so tired and I feel mentally numb. I don't know how much longer I can take this. Does his plan include killing me after I've given him a child? I push the thought away. I have an image of him keeping me here even if I'm dead. He would probably still wash my corpse.

How much longer do I have to endure this nightmare? I have to pee in a bucket in the corner of the room. William happily empties it every day after inhaling the aroma. I have to endure his bony hands washing my face every morning. This morning, the sponge went around my neck and down towards my chest. Each morning he moves the sponge lower.

I need to sleep. Life always seems easier after a good sleep. Then I will think about how to escape. Hopefully, my dreams will show me a way out. A premonition. With any luck, it will involve killing the pair of them.

Feeling sleepy, my mind begins to drift. I feel calm and my body begins to warm slightly in the thin blanket.

"Faith, are you asleep?"

It's William. I didn't hear him come in. I pause before answering.

"If you thought I was sleeping, why are you talking to me, you idiot?" I snap. So much for not antagonising the enemy.

"Now, now. Calm down. Be a good girl. I've got you some beef stew to warm you up."

"Go away, William. I'm not eating it, it's probably poisoned."

My response is full of aggression. He is studying me.

"It's not. Look, I'll try some."

His bony fingers hold the spoon as he sucks up a spoonful of stew. His teeth are brown and I doubt he's ever been to a dentist. The stew does smell good and my stomach aches with hunger or is it from the bitter cold? I only get two meals a day. Usually toast for breakfast and soup for the evening meal. I watch as William eats another spoonful. Convinced it is safe to eat, I slowly sit up straight on the bed with the blanket still around me, trying to capture some warmth. I hold out my left hand and he hands me the stew. The warmth of the bowl feels like heaven to my cold fingers. I eat hungrily and it tastes fine.

"Thank you."

Ironically, I feel grateful to him.

"That's all right, Dear. You can have some more tomorrow, if you're good. Mother said the iron will be good for you. Sleep well. Goodnight."

He leaves, locking the door once again.

I sleep well, grateful for the warm meal inside me. The cold is getting me down.

*

It's morning and I don't object when William carries out the usual routine of washing my face and hands, cleaning my teeth and brushing my hair.

"You're quiet this morning, my dear. Are you all right?"

He sounds genuinely concerned.

"All right? Am I all right? I have no clothing. This stinking room is freezing. I'm being kept here by you, and you ask me if I'm all right. You need locking up. You're a danger to yourself."

I'm so angry, the words just tumble out.

"I'm growing tired of you being rude to me. You're a naughty girl and naughty girls must be punished. I am going to tell Mother. You will have no more food today. I should send you to your room for being such a naughty girl, but you're already here."

He is laughing to himself. I hear the bolt as he locks the door.

"Bastard," I yell after him.

I'm so cold. I need to plan my escape. I've spent many hours shouting for help from the only window in this room but no one has ever called back. Will I ever be free? My poor parents will be so worried. Frustration is rapidly turning to anger and I can feel my volatile temper consuming me.

Fuck this. I've had enough.

Jumping from the tattered bed, I pound my fists against the bedroom door.

"WILLIAM. WILLIAM. LET ME OUT. NOW. I'VE HAD ENOUGH. I AM FREEZING COLD. PLEASE."

I scream the words and my high-pitched wail hurts my ears. Abruptly, the door opens. I don't manage to step back in time and it hits my leg but I'm okay.

"Stop screaming. You'll wake Mother. She is having a nap."

William is agitated and his voice is just a little more than a whisper. He doesn't like his mother being disturbed.

"I don't care."

My voice is still raised and anger now consumes me.

"I am freezing cold. I want some clothes."

"Well, you can't. You'll only try to escape."

He's shaking his head at me. I wish I had a knife so that I could stab him. Multiple times.

"I want something warm to wear, you dick-head."

I hate being cold. I hate the disgusting smell of the blanket I'm forced to pull tightly around my thin frame.

"Right," snarls William. "You want something warm to wear. I'll give you something warm to wear and you'll bloody well wear it."

He's really pissed off. I don't know what he's about to do. He storms off and I am a little taken aback. He is usually calm. Have I gone too far this time? He's so precious about his mother. I dismiss the thought. I want my freedom and behaving like this is a way to wear him down. If I keep waking his precious mother up, he might let me go or forget to bolt the door.

The door swings open. It's wide open. He's feeling confident that I'm not going to flee.

"Here," he says, and he has a sickening look of triumph about him. "Here is something to keep you warm. It's a hat. Mother stitched it, especially for you."

He throws the hat on the bed. No, it can't be. I pray that my eyes are deceiving me. No, he couldn't have. Even he can't be that sick. Slowly I reach out my hand and pick it up gently. It has a metallic smell. It's covered in dry blood yet the smooth soft touch feels so familiar. His mother has taken something that I love and defiled it. It's Snowy, my cat.

The bastard has stolen my cat and crudely skinned her, then sewn her soft raven-black fur around a woollen hat. Hugging the remains of my slaughtered cat tightly to my face, for the first time since being here, I start to cry. Soft silent tears fall onto her fur. I'm heartbroken. This is the worst moment of my life.

Sadly, my instinct is telling me there is much worse to come.

*

William stood in silence, watching her, and displeasure showed on his face. That was not the reaction he wanted. Her angry outbursts excited him as it meant she had lost control. He was always in control. As he stood watching, he felt uncomfortable. He felt sorry for her. That was a new feeling for him.

She was rocking backwards and forwards, holding the remains of her cat. Shocked by her reaction, he quietly left the room. He had not meant to hurt her. In his sick mind, it was just a game. He wanted Faith to be dependent on him. To fall in love with him. Victims often fall in love with their captors.

He was sure that Helen had loved him. She had stayed locked in that room for five years. No one missed her or came looking for her. Eventually, he had grown tired of feeding and cleaning her. She was often ill with colds and sickness. She had stopped fighting back and was no fun anymore. She had never given him a child. Tired of her compliance, Mother had stabbed her. She had lain, buried in their garden, for two years. It was so overgrown. William only occasionally remembered that she was there.

Briefly, he remembered the fateful day. Mother had enjoyed taking the young girl's life as he watched. He always loved to watch. His job was to dispose of her. Despite being heavy, he had managed to drag her downstairs and into the grave he had dug a few days before. He recalled how his back had ached, after filling the deep hole with soil. He hoped Mother had killed her because he didn't check her pulse before dumping her into the ground on top of his father's remains. He couldn't even remember her surname.

But he had no intention of letting Faith go. His mother wanted grandchildren badly and Faith had to give her them.

His mother told him that when she died, he would be lonely, and he would need a daughter to take care of him.

Seeing Faith so upset puzzled William. He knew what to do to make her happy. He would get her a companion and he knew just the lady. And so did Faith.

Chapter Seven

Imogen Fernsby sat at her desk in her busy office trying to do the follow-up piece on the missing girl. It had been ten days since she had disappeared and no one had come forward and no body had been found.

At least, that is something.

She stared at the piece she was trying to type but the words she needed escaped her. The only new information was that the girl's cat had disappeared.

Big deal.

If she was honest with herself, it was Aidan Handford she was mad at, not the missing girl. They had hardly spoken over the last few days. Imogen knew they had a casual relationship but was still hurt that he had arranged to go to dinner with the missing girl. He hadn't been out since he had learnt about Faith's disappearance. She wondered what had really been going on between them.

The vibration from her mobile, followed by a burst of 'The Waltz' ringtone, broke her thoughts. She answered without checking the caller's ID.

"Hello, Imogen Fernsby speaking."

"Hi, it's me."

Imogen recognised the voice immediately. Her heart started to thump. Her hands felt clammy.

"Hi, Aidan. What do you want?"

Be mean to him. He deserves it.

"We need to talk. Will you meet me for dinner tonight?"

She felt a surge of excitement but, this time, she wasn't going to let Aidan walk all over her.

"No, sorry I can't. I've made plans," she lied.

"Okay, what about lunch today?"

"Sorry, can't make lunch either. I've got too much work to do. You know the sort of thing, like finding your missing girlfriend."

You bitch, she thought, smiling a little to herself as she imagined Aidan squirming at the other end of the telephone.

"She wasn't my girlfriend. She was a friend," he protested.

"Until the end of the night. I know you, Aidan, and I've decided I don't want to see you anymore. You're never there for me but I'm expected to always be there for you. It's not fair."

She said the words even though she didn't mean a word of them.

"Please meet me for dinner tonight. I have something important to tell you."

"No. Goodbye, Aidan. I'm too busy, sorry."

She ended the call.

She loved him so much and hated to argue with him but she wanted commitment. Life was too short to keep hanging on to people. But it didn't stop her from feeling terrible.

Staring back at her laptop, she re-read her piece on the girl and wondered.

Where are you? I'm going to find you. Then we'll see what Aidan has to say.

She decided to visit Faith's workplace and interview her boss. Flicking through her notes, she came across his name. Mr Evans.

Right, Mr Evans. I'll be with you in half an hour.

*

Imogen immediately liked the look of Mr Evans and was very impressed that he came out of a meeting to see her.

"Hello, Mr Evans. My name is Imogen Fernsby. Thank you very much for seeing me at such short notice."

"That's all right. When the temporary secretary told me you were here, I wondered if it was news about Faith," he replied hopefully. "I've told the police everything I can remember about that day. It was just a normal day."

"Nothing new I'm afraid," she said as she took a seat in the reception area where Mr Evans indicated.

"Did Faith get on well with all the staff?" she asked.

"We are a team. Well, yes, I think so. I'm sure she was very popular. She was always being invited out by them."

Imogen grimaced as she briefly thought of one member of staff in particular, but she didn't let it show. Fifteen minutes later, she thanked Mr Evans for his time and promised to let him know of any news.

"If you do find her, tell her that her job is still here."

"That is very kind of you."

She left the office building feeling frustrated by the lack of new information. She knew how the police felt. They had searched the area and interviewed Faith's work colleagues and they were still no further forward. She stood for a moment, people-watching. No one glanced her way. The chill in the air caught your breath so, wrapped up warmly, people hurried along. It was only September, yet various coats, hats and scarves were all doing the same thing.

It was an odd feeling, knowing that Faith had previously walked down the same street where she now stood.

But which way did she go? Had she walked or did she get into a car?

51

They hadn't even met. Faith didn't know Imogen existed but, to her, Faith was becoming an obsession. The police had traced her usual route home. They had even spoken to the few remaining occupants of a rundown housing estate, which was near to her way home. Most properties stood boarded-up and empty. No one had seen her.

Imogen had only been away from the office for just under two hours but was glad to be back. As she approached her desk, she stopped. Lying on it was a huge bouquet. She knew who it was from but she still opened the card attached. It read:

Imogen, sorry. I messed up. Love you, A xxxx

She was ecstatic. In all the years she had known Aidan, he had never said he loved her. Picking up the phone, she hastily dialled his number. He answered after the second ring. She asked him only one question.

"What time is dinner tonight?"

He could hear from her voice that she was smiling. He was just relieved to be out of her bad books. He didn't want to blow their friendship but commitment terrified him. He loved his freedom and other women too much but he didn't want to lose her. Maybe he could have both; marriage and discreet times with one or two others.

Imogen dressed very carefully for dinner that night. She had finished work early and had gone shopping. She had seen the dress she wanted immediately, which was very unusual as it normally took her hours of shopping to find something she liked. But not that day. The dress she picked was red. She had chosen deliberately as it was the colour she wore on the night she had first met Aidan. Only this time, instead of being short, it was long with a split running up to her left thigh.

Perfect.

Back home, she'd had a long bath, painted her nails and set her long brunette hair in rollers. She left her hair down, a mass of sexy curls, and the result was amazing. Her makeup emphasised her good looks and, for once, Imogen was pleased with the result. She had half an hour to spare; time for a glass of wine. She headed to the kitchen to pour the first of the night before the cab came to pick her up.

At Aidan's house, the situation was much the same. He had even gone out from work and bought himself a new grey shirt, to go with a dark grey suit jacket and jeans. His shoes had been polished until they shone and his hair had been tidied up by a trip to the barbers on the way home.

Standing back to admire his reflection in the bathroom mirror, he was pleased with what he saw but, then again, Aidan usually was. Imogen would often tease him about being vain which he furiously denied, even to himself.

Aidan arrived first at the restaurant. It was Italian; Imogen's favourite food. The walls were painted a deep rich red with a green border which gave the feeling of opulence. Pictures of Italy hung from the walls. There was soft music playing and red tealight candles burning in small glasses on each of the fifteen tables. The smell of garlic made him feel hungry. The waiter showed him to their table. Imogen was ten minutes late. Feeling inside his jacket, it was safe there. Imogen's gift. This would change everything between them. He felt nervous as if it was their first date. The waiter appeared with the wine list and he ordered a bottle of house red; anything for the waiter to leave him in peace.

He sat staring at the wine. Was he making the right decision? Then he saw her. He thought she looked amazing. Waving as she saw him, she headed immediately in his direction, not even noticing the waiter who had come forward to escort her to their table.

"You look gorgeous."

He felt proud of her. He wasn't going to forget this night.

"You don't look bad yourself," she joked, as she took her seat opposite him.

They laughed and joked throughout the meal. They both ordered healthy and very tasty gnocchi with hazelnut pesto and butternut squash. The light-hearted atmosphere ended when the waiter interrupted them by placing a bottle of pre-ordered champagne on their table.

"What's this for?" asked Imogen, eyeing the champagne. "We've already nearly drunk two bottles of wine."

"Imogen, I have something to ask you but I don't know how to."

"What is it?"

She felt uneasy.

What has he done now?

"Oh, I don't know how to do this. Here, this is for you. I hope it's okay."

He removed the gift he had bought earlier that day from his inside pocket. A very attractive assistant had helped him choose it. He didn't think, under the circumstances, that it was appropriate to ask for her number.

Opening the small blue-velvet jewellery box, tears sprung to Imogen's eyes. The diamond engagement ring was small and tasteful. She never thought this moment would come.

"Oh, Aidan."

"Oh, one other thing," said Aidan. "Will you marry me?"

Imogen leapt from her chair and hugged him. She was so happy.

Everything does come to those who wait.

*

They left the restaurant hand in hand, discussing their future together. They didn't notice the figure who had been standing, watching the restaurant from a shady doorway opposite. The same figure who had been following Aidan for a few days. He had a trilby hat pulled down low over his eyes and a grey trench coat was the only barrier he had against the cold night air. He'd been waiting patiently for them to leave. Watching them giggling like children.

How dare he? He doesn't deserve to have Faith as a friend. This scene would upset her. I'll have to take care of it.

The newly-engaged couple were discussing where to live. They would sell their flats and buy a house together. A three-bedroom house, ready for the day they would have children. Two would be a good number. They planned to marry within six months at a registry office with only a select number of family and close friends present.

Aidan felt happy. Until that moment he had not wanted commitment. The thought of it made him feel suffocated. But he loved Imogen, in his own way, and realised he had taken her for granted. When Faith disappeared he'd been shocked, but the thought of anything happening to Imogen had scared him. It was then that he realised he did love her and could no longer deny the fact. He had liked Faith and would have gone on a few dates with her if she hadn't disappeared but, at that moment, he was glad he hadn't.

High, on the atmosphere of the night and house wine, he stepped near the edge of the kerb to flag down a cab. The road was busy but he could see a cab five or six cars back. He didn't see the stranger in the grey trench coat walk silently up behind him. He just felt the force of the shove as he fell forwards and his head hit the oncoming car. The impact sent him over the bonnet onto the road. He landed with a sickening thud, but he was still alive. The second car, travelling in the opposite direction, hit the brakes a split second too late. Aidan disappeared under the second car, a large 4-wheeled BMW.

Imogen had seen it all but was unable to move, unable to cry out. Instead, she had stood and watched.

Chapter Eight

William marked off day 13 on his calendar.

Faith had been living with him and his mother for thirteen days. A smile crossed his face as he thought of his dear mother; so loving, loyal and kind. Faith would be the same one day. She would grow to love him. He was sure. Mother said she would.

He rose extra early that morning as he had a long day ahead. A day that excited him. It stirred up old feelings. An adrenaline rush consumed him as he pictured the danger of the situation that was about to unfold. Taking in another 'guest' to share Faith's room would surely make her happy.

Mother wasn't happy at first because of the extra mouth to feed. They usually only had one meal a day, supper. Sometimes they'd have breakfast if there was any bread to make toast. But once he explained his plan clearly to her, she gave him her blessing. Extra food wouldn't be necessary. Pleased with himself, he dressed quickly, not bothering to wash. That was a regular occurrence for William as he only washed before he ate supper.

This time he'd need to take the car. It wasn't registered to him or even taxed or insured. He didn't bother with society's rules. It had belonged to a neighbour who had died about eight years ago. No one took the car away and no one claimed it. It had just been left parked in the street after the undertaker took away the deceased, so William had broken into the house and helped himself to the car keys and a pair of shoes. There was nothing else worth taking.

There was only one other occupied house near by and William was a regular visitor. That of the drug dealer, 23-year-old Craig Jones, who supplied him with Ketamine from time to time. William told him that his mother used it when her constant aches and pains were bad.

*

The room has grown dark. The cold chill never seems to change, it's unyielding. I dread the daytime but I dread nights more. I watch the strange shapes of darkness. Sometimes I see people standing utterly still, watching me. Are my tired eyes playing tricks? The imaginary shapes stir memories of my childhood when, from the comfort of my bed, I would have peeped out from behind my feather quilt to look at the shapes on the bedroom curtains. I thought I could see faces, so many faces, before throwing the quilt quickly over my head again.

Only, this time, I am not a child. Nor do I even have a cosy quilt. I am extremely tired, cold and fearful for my life. But how can I escape? No one comes to the house. I've never heard anyone outside the window. My dreams, when I do sleep, are either filled with freedom, walking along a beach with miles of golden sand ahead, or the other dream where I brutally murder William. I drift off to sleep, thinking of the latter.

*

When I wake, I don't notice the cold room, the lack of clothes or the isolation. Instead, I feel determination and inner strength. Today, something is going to be different. I sense something is going to change. Maybe I'm going to regain my freedom. Gone are the usual feelings of helplessness and frustration. Today, I feel will bring an ending and a new beginning in my life.

"William! William!" I bawl.

William opens the door. I don't give him any time to speak.

"I've been thinking. Seeing this is now my new home I would like to add a few personal touches to my room."

I smile at him. Taken slightly aback by the sudden, but pleasant, change in my attitude, William smiles. Confident that I am coming around to his way of thinking.

She will be a better mother to the child I plan to have with her if she is content and happy. She was drugged and oblivious to our union on her first night. It wasn't enjoyable, as I like them to be awake. As usual, Mother had helped by holding her down. She usually enjoys watching me but she had told me to hurry up. Tonight, I will make sure she gets pregnant.

I am not sure what he is thinking but I continue with my false smile.

"What do you have in mind?"

He is intrigued.

"Well, I thought maybe a warm dry blanket, some clean sheets for the bed and some kind of heating, if possible," I ask, hopefully. "And, if it's not too much trouble, I'd like a newspaper or magazine to read."

I could see him, studying me intently.

She is so pretty. Maybe when Mother has gone, she will make a good wife. I don't like to think of Mother as gone. I love her too much. Or do I? She has controlled me all my life. I remember the beatings she gave me as a child, if I upset her. She still lashes out but old age has weakened the blows. When she does pass, all I will have left in the world is Faith and she will surely love me then. Won't she? I think she is warming to me.

"I will see what I can do. I will be back shortly with your breakfast."

He leaves the room and then reappears, as promised, with food. He carries the usual battered tray, displaying the usual breakfast. Two slices of toast, tea mixed with Ketamine and, this time, sleeping pills in a chipped dirty mug. But, this morning, there is something extra for breakfast. A newspaper.

I desperately try not to look smug.

I thank him and he leaves without another word. Thankfully, he hasn't bothered to wash my hands and face this morning.

His mind is elsewhere. There is an excitement bubbling within him.

I eat my toast but throw the tea on the floor, in the corner near the window. William never notices as it just mixes in with the rest of the stains. The only other liquid is the glass of water I was given at supper.

If he comes in soon, I will pretend to be asleep. This has happened before. He stands, watching me, thinking I am in a drugged sleep. He strokes my hair and kisses my face. His breath is rancid against my skin.

I open the newspaper as quietly as I can. It's from over a week ago. That's okay as I don't want it to read. It's the key to the way out of here. I wonder if I've been in the papers lately. Have my poor parents had to provide a recent photo for the media? Has my disappearance gone viral?

My disappearance has made the local paper. The article on page ten states the police investigation continues and my parents have made an appeal for my return on the local news. They both look drawn and exhausted.

It is comforting to know they are looking for me.

After reading the newspaper from cover to cover, I carefully fold it back up again. I don't know how long I was reading but I relish the normality of doing so. There is nothing particularly interesting. Mortgage rates are expected to change, petrol prices have risen slightly and a family have been killed abroad but no arrests have been made. To me, this newspaper is priceless.

*

For the third time that day, William appears in my room. I lie still and pretend to be asleep.

"This is for you."

He places something next to me. I pretend to be a little disorientated as I wake to the sound of his voice. Slowly I sit up.

I look at the gift and keep all expressions carefully from my face. Inwardly, I grin. No, not grin, I'm laughing my head off! Strangely, I feel grateful. I wrap myself in the blue woollen blanket. It's not new but it doesn't smell of pee. For a cherished split second, I envisage myself back at home. I remember the child I used to be, climbing into a clean bed after a Sunday night bath, before school the next morning.

Opening my eyes ends the fantasy. He is stroking my hair. I brace myself as I know he'll start kissing my face soon. I switch off my mind. Instead, I focus on the dirty off-white flannelette sheet and, now, the blue blanket that covers my body. Such a stark contrast between them.

I can't take any more. I move my head from his sickening touch. I can smell him. I can smell his body odour, a stench of sweat and filth.

"I have another surprise for you."

I am not expecting him to say that as he moves towards the door to retrieve whatever it is from the passage. Bingo! He places a very old and battered heater in front of me.

"It does work. It is from my room but you can borrow it for a couple of days unless you would like me to keep you warm?"

His eyes are boring into me.

"I'm sure it will be fine, thank you."

I force a smile. It's clear from his tone what he has in mind. I feel sick and terrified at the same time.

Lulled into a false sense of security and feeling that he has won my trust, he decides to collect payment. Taking my head in his hands, he kisses me full on the mouth. Then he slowly licks the left side of my face and his hand wanders to my right breast.

"Stop it, stop it."

I can't believe what he has just done. I know he can do much worse but not now, not today. I have my escape planned.

I'm afraid and I start to lash out. My left fist connects with his jaw. He grabs me by the throat. I don't want to die! He's squeezing tightly. I can't breathe. He lets go with one hand to slap me across my face. It stings and I bounce off the bed. I'm no longer covered by the dirty sheet or my new blue blanket. I'm exposed on the grubby floor in my underwear. I dare not move. I can feel my heart beating. It's beating so fast.

"You ungrateful bitch!"

He's coming for me. Grabbing my hair, he roughly hauls me from the floor. His hands have found my neck again. He is squeezing hard. Is this it? Is this the day I die? I open my eyes and stare defiantly into his. His eyes are wild and blazing with anger. I can feel a twinge in his trousers. He's turned on. He feels powerful and feels in charge. I fight to breathe. He lets go and I collapse to the floor, gasping for breath.

"You will pay for that. No supper for you."

He is breathing heavily too. I hear him storm from the room. He's livid and probably thinks I'm ungrateful. He has snatched the blanket back but has left the heater. Like a naughty child, I will be punished by having no supper. Again, he's asserting his power over me.

I stay on the floor shocked and bruised. I slowly move my head to look for the sheet to cover myself. It's within arm's reach so I wrap it around me tighter than usual for some small comfort.

Tonight, I will either regain my freedom or I will die. I don't care if it's the latter. I'd rather die than give him a child. Hunger and thirst are taking their toll. I've lost weight and my mouth is permanently dry. I'm living on about one glass of water and some soup a day.

*

William stormed back to his bedroom which was the same as the rest of the house; dirty and damp as his mother never cleaned. Next to his bed, which he regularly wet – a habit he had never grown out of since childhood, was a stack of adult magazines. He had read these from the tender age of six. As a child, his mother had never bought him comics that most little boys like to read and pretend they are superheroes. He was given adult magazines. His father died when he was four years old. That was when the beatings started. But, with his father gone, he got to sleep in his mother's bed.

It was not his magazine collection that interested him now. It was the dead body lying on his bed. His new lodger.

She had lost her life only two hours ago when William had placed his hands tightly around her throat. Strangulation was not an easy task. His arms ached.

He'd only been watching her for a few days and decided this was the day to take her. She was walking next to a park, where Mother was pretending to be lost.

No one is ever suspicious of an elderly woman. It works every time.

Walking to the car, on the pretence of getting a pen and paper to write down directions, he went behind her and injected her with a mixture of Ketamine and sleeping pills. He then put her in the back of the car quickly before raising any suspicion.

He had set her body on his bed, in a peaceful sleeping position. She lay on her side with her face turned towards the door. The skin tone had lost its pink glow. The body, still clothed, looked waxy. The neck showed bruising.

William found strangulation hard work but exhilarating. In the movies, people died quickly but, in his experience, it took about ten minutes. He liked to practise when he could. He tenderly brushed the dark hair away from the lifeless face. He would wash her. Then tonight, while Mother slept, he would cuddle the body. The thought excited him.

He had planned to let her live and stay in Faith's room. But now, he would place her next to Faith when she was in a drugged sleep, in the early hours of the morning. When she awoke, she would have a companion. William knew she would be pleased.

But she didn't deserve company after hitting him, so the body would have to stay in his room for a couple of hours. He started to undress her.

I might as well have some pleasure.

*

The days imprisoned here are long but the nights are longer. I lie in fear of him creeping into my room at night. I have memories of his naked body on mine the first night I was here. I remember his mother's voice but the memories are blurred. Did he rape me or was it a dream?

Tonight, I feel no fear; only inner calm. The room, for once, feels slightly warmer. Time has no meaning here but I think it's been about an hour since I heard the voices of William and his mother. He must have been in his room.

I can hear him at my door. Pretending to be asleep, I lie very still with my back to the door. My heart is pounding with the thought that he might put his bony fingers on me again.

He's in my room, dragging something heavy. I remain still so that he thinks I'm in another drugged sleep. He must not find out that I no longer drink the tea. I don't know what he keeps giving me, but it is harder to function and focus each day.

I feel the bed shift and I think he's lying down beside me. I can feel something touch my back but it feels cold. I remain still.

Footsteps head towards the door. I'm confused when I hear the bolt sliding back but I can feel something or someone lying very close behind me. If it is someone, they are making no sound.

Listening intently, I hear the familiar sound of a door being slammed shut. I think it must be William's room. If he has left the room, who is next to me? Slowly I turn my body towards the cold form I feel against my exposed skin. The room is dark, only lit by the nearly-full moon that shines through the dirty window.

The person is lying on her back, naked. Brown hair frames her lifeless face. A face that used to hold an alluring smile is now expressionless and sunken. Tentatively, I touch her unnaturally cold cheek. Removing the only sheet I have from my lower legs, I cover her nakedness. Deep ugly bruises cover her neck.

He has strangled Rebecca Bixby. My best friend.

When I do eradicate William, it is going to be long and exceptionally painful. For a moment, I rest my head on her chest. I feel numb. I don't know if it's the drugs or the shock.

My beautiful friend. Gone.

Before I climb off the bed, I kiss Rebecca's forehead. I tell her I love her and say my goodbyes. Now is not the time for emotion as I need to focus.

I start to remove small pieces of the hideous orange and brown wallpaper from the damp walls. It's an appeasing exercise. Making a small pile on the bed next to Rebecca, I pick up each of the six pieces, taking my time to slightly crumble each one. I pile them on top of each other and make a small tower. I remove the newspaper from under the bed and tear it as quietly as I can into thick strips. Carefully, and taking my time, I fold over the top corner into a triangle, then continue turning over and folding more triangles. They are no longer flimsy pieces of newspaper, they are concertina firelighters. I give each one a little pull to stretch them out. Flames will spread slowly through the concertinas, giving me plenty of time to commit arson. I push the thought of Rebecca from my mind. I'm about to burn the body of my best friend.

Sitting in front of the electric heater, I insert the firelighters into the vents on the front. They start to smoke but there are no flames. Damn. Come on, come on.

Gently, I blow on them. They smell of burning. A flame appears, then another and another. I take the wallpaper and calmly use the flames to light each one and then I drop them onto the carpet.

Removing the bedsheet from Rebecca's body, I'm about to discover if it is fire-retardant. If it isn't, it will ignite and burn out in about 32 seconds. I remember watching a fire-safety video at school. Handy when your life is at stake from a stalker. Handy because I'm doing everything the video told us not to do.

The smoke is stinging my eyes. I add the corner of the bedsheet and it slowly starts to burn. The fire is starting to spread. I've draped the burning sheet on the bed and it starts to burn ferociously. A small fire has turned into a major fire. I can't put this out, even if I want to. It's hot but no longer as bright. The room is even darker as black smoke starts to rise. I drop to my knees and head to the door.

This isn't going as planned. The fire is intensifying. Toxic gases make taking a breath hurt. If I don't get out in the next minute, I will die from the smoke.

"FIRE, FIRE."

I bang on the door as hard as my lungs allow.

"WILLIAM! WILLIAM!"

I hear the familiar sliding sound of the bolt being pulled back. I crawl back a little to allow the door to open. Aware that it is holding the fire back, I brace myself. This red beast is about to get a big hit of oxygen and grow in size and intensity. I throw myself through the gap, into the passage. Glancing back quickly, I see William duck down before he slams the door shut.

"What have you done?"

He shrieks the words but I don't answer. I need to find a way out but I'm unfamiliar with the layout. Smoke is thick in the air. William only has one thing on his mind.

"MOTHER, MOTHER!"

I head for the stairs, my legs buckling from weakness, or is it the smoke that invades my lungs? I'm nearly at the bottom and I can see the front door. The door I entered many days ago. The door that changed my life. It's bolted and locked. I can't see a key. There's smoke coming from the ceiling and it is suffocating.

William is stumbling on the stairs. He has his mother in his arms. His face is thunderous. If he gets to me, he'll kill me before the smoke does.

"Come here, you little bitch!"

He's nearly at the bottom. His mother isn't moving. I hope she's dead.

Desperate to escape, I crawl along the floor into the front room. I don't want to pass out. I don't want to die a victim. I'm not a victim.

Overcome with inner strength and steely determination to survive, I stand and pick up a small wooden table. I hurl it towards the window. There's a crack but it hasn't broken. The frames are wooden. I know, as I've stared out of a similar window, incarcerated for hours. I've studied these windows. Single-glazed and very draughty. I search around the floor. My hands hit something heavy which feels like a sewing machine.

It's my last chance as I'm suffocating. I pick up the heavy object and throw it with all my strength. The exploding sound of shattering glass fills my ears. I don't hesitate. I throw myself through the jagged shards of the portal. My head connects sharply with the ground below and my right shoulder is gashed open. Landing with a heavy thud, I black out.

Chapter Nine
Mother's Story

William's mother, Elizabeth, was the oldest of the three children of Ruth and Charles Winter. Young Elizabeth never went hungry and always had a pretty dress but she had lacked attention. Her mother, Ruth, was a seamstress by day and went out drinking with her father by night. Her parents never let being responsible for three children mar their fun. As a child, she always felt there was no room for her in their relationship. She couldn't remember either of them hugging her, they were absorbed in each other.

She'd help herself to food in the fridge, put herself to bed at night and get herself up in the morning. Neither parent noticed, nor was particularly bothered if she went to school which most days she didn't. Ruth preferred a lie-in to the school run.

Elizabeth's youngest sibling, Natalie, spent most of her time hanging out with her friends, discovering alcohol at eleven and drugs the year after. At twenty-three, Natalie had her only child, Abbey. But drugs and children didn't work together. One dominated the other, so baby Abbey went to live and be raised by their middle sister, Dorothy, who never had children of her own after her husband, Richard 'Rich' Heist, passed at thirty-one. Dorothy Heist, or Dot as she preferred to be called, had been raised by their grandparents who insisted that she attended school.

Elizabeth rarely saw or wanted anything to do with her siblings. She hadn't seen either of them in about forty years.

Her school thought it was odd that two of the sisters attended but not the other. However, some of the teachers felt it was easier when Elizabeth, with her cold ways, wasn't in their classroom. Even Natalie attended school at times, along with her hangover.

Elizabeth's parents remained emotionally unavailable so she grew up to be guarded, angry and hostile. Neither of them showed tolerance towards her, so she learnt how to squash emotions and, sadly, became an emotionally cold, unsmiling and secretive young adult. She didn't need anybody and thought others were insignificant compared to her unique self.

Her world changed at the age of eighteen, as she stood at a bus stop. She didn't know it at the time but the young man who struck up a conversation with her would become her future husband. He was Alfred William Channing, a quiet young man who showed her kindness. He adored her and Elizabeth was finally the centre of attention and cared for. She was impressed by his good looks and tall stature. Physically, she committed to their relationship but emotionally she stayed unavailable. That was her way of ensuring she avoided the painful sting of rejection.

They married eight months later in the local registry office with only his parents in attendance, Edward and Doris. Elizabeth didn't invite any of her family. A few drinks followed the small ceremony in the function room at their local pub, the White Swan.

It was in the same function room, a short time later, where a wake was held for Alfred's parents who suddenly passed, only days apart. Alfred was devastated. They had suffered from debilitating stomach pains, fever and vomiting. Their doctor was baffled and the hospital thought it was appendicitis or gallstones. Finally, they said it was some type of virus.

Elizabeth knew it was phosphide poisoning, otherwise known as rat poison. She had made and dropped off the casserole which had been laced with it. She was intrigued to see if she had put enough in and how long it would take to work. The answer was yes and it took six days for Doris and eight for Edward. But they had to go. Elizabeth didn't like her husband to be close to anyone.

Alfred inherited some money which he insisted on keeping in the bank for their future. Knowing she was responsible for their deaths gave her a warm glow inside. She liked having a shocking secret. It had been so easy. She wanted to do it again. She wondered how it would feel to murder someone up close. She started to make a mental note of potential victims.

To make sure she had a well-thought-out plan for when she killed again, she asked Alfred to build a large shed in the garden. She told him it was to grow herbs. At first, he was confused. Their garden was overgrown and the earth was not flat. But on weekends, if he wasn't working as a postman, he levelled it off, throwing piles of rocks and earth to the side. Elizabeth insisted on plastic sheeting for the floor, not wood. Wood rots she told him and he obliged. Anything to keep her happy, as she unnerved him when she was annoyed with him, which was usually whenever he was at home.

She got her shed. That made her happy. Her own private space. With Albert at work during the week, she cut back the thick plastic floor and started digging his grave.

Despite Alfred very quickly regretting marrying the aloof, impersonal and hostile Elizabeth, William Alfred Channing was born nearly two years later. Their only child. Elizabeth hated being pregnant and hated giving birth even more. It was the most excruciating pain she'd ever experienced. She thought she would die. Once the baby had been delivered safely, she had wanted to kick the smiling, caring midwife's face in as she had not enjoyed being in control.

Rose had been a midwife for fifteen years and was relieved when Mrs Channing's labour was over. She had also found the seven-hour labour draining. She had not enjoyed being in the company of the cold aloof first-time mother. When Elizabeth looked at her son, only minutes old, she felt nothing.

William vividly remembered his mother yelling at his father in the kitchen when he was about four years old. He remembered Mother picking up the knife and sticking it in Father's chest. There was a lot of red on Father and the floor but Mother was livid and she kept sticking the knife in. Over and over and over. Mother often got angry and would yell at him or throw things at Father. At times, Father would get cross too and throw things back. That was when William went and lay under his bed until it got dark or the house went quiet. Even as an adult, he still felt fearful when others got angry.

He never saw Father after that day in the kitchen. Mother said he'd gone away to work but he knew that was a lie. Father was in the garden in a big hole inside Mother's shed. He never told her that he knew as he didn't want to end up in that hole. Mother never mentioned Father again.

She never looked sad but she rarely smiled so it was hard to tell what she was feeling. She didn't go to work and spent her days in front of the television, humming to herself. Sometimes she would knit William a jumper but they were always too tight and too short. Once Father disappeared,

William cuddled up to Mother and slept in her bed. He continued to do this regularly throughout his adult life.

His mother's parenting skills consisted of abandonment, neglect and mistreatment of poor William. The more she pushed him away emotionally, the tighter he clung. Her emotional coldness grew stronger. She remembered with irritation how she had been expected to take him to school and how he'd moan for food daily. And the clothes, how quickly he'd outgrow them.

Eventually, she stopped taking him to school and somehow the authorities stopped chasing him, so William spent his childhood at home, keeping out of his mother's way. His imagination was his only friend. There, he had another mother who wrapped him in affection, love and praise. He imagined that one day she would knock on the door and take him away. He liked to pretend that Mother had pinched him from the hospital. He had spent his whole life trying to please her. Wanting her to love him.

Elizabeth preferred motherhood after she had stabbed her husband to death. She could still remember that day. The metallic smell of his blood, the knife plunging back and forth, occasionally bending as it hit his breastbone. Having to keep a tight grip on the blade as the blood made the handle slip. The attack was so frenzied that the end of the blade broke.

She had pictured her parents as she plunged that knife into her husband. Seeing him lying on the kitchen floor made her feel powerful. She remembered waiting for it to get dark before she dragged the body, with a strength that came from deep within, into the hole in the garden which she had dug years before. None of them used the garden. William wasn't allowed outside and her husband purposely spent most of his time at work.

She distinctly remembered her euphoria as she dragged and pushed that body into the muddy hole. She didn't fill it in immediately. She waited for a few days. Choosing instead to sneak out when it was dark to stare at the body. It made her smile.

Cleaning the kitchen was another matter. The smell of her dead husband seemed to linger for many weeks. She liked the fact that she would be making a cup of tea in the kitchen, knowing that his blood was directly under her feet, soaked into the cracks of the brown patterned vinyl. She wasn't sure why she ended up disliking him so much. There wasn't anything in particular, only that he had existed.

*

Once he was gone, William had no one to complain to that he was hungry or that his trousers were too short. He didn't want to end up in the hole. He had bad dreams about the hole. He used to dream that his father was climbing out of it, angry and covered in blood. Walking through the walls of their house to seek revenge.

He would wake terrified and try to snuggle into his mother. She would push him away, even in her sleep. William could remember being four years old and watching from the window as his mother dragged a large dark shape across the garden. The garden he was never allowed to play in. Once Alfred was dead, Elizabeth didn't hide her lack of intolerance towards the child.

When William was six, Elizabeth stopped taking him to school. She never went to school, so couldn't see the point in the hassle of getting him there. Then there were the other parents and the odd looks they gave her. It might have been from pity as they knew her husband had abandoned her. He'd run off with a woman he had got pregnant. Elizabeth knew the rumour, as she had started it.

She didn't know why she had killed three people. She just knew she had enjoyed it and afterwards she felt such a release. It felt powerful, knowing that one day the hole she'd dug in the garden would become her husband's grave.

Other than his parents' inheritance, which was still in the bank, she had nothing to gain financially as she had to pretend he'd run off. What she did gain was freedom. Freedom to mould William to do the things she fantasised about.

It was Albert's fault she'd poisoned his parents. He had been too close to them. His parents cared about him and she didn't like that. She felt they thought she wasn't good enough for their only son. She saw herself as the victim, raised by parents who had no time for her, no friends at school and even her sisters didn't care.

But she was concerned that William would be left with no one once she'd gone. She hadn't been to a doctor in years but she knew something was wrong with her health. The tightness in her chest, shortness of breath and, at times, numbness in her legs. She felt she may not have long left in this world. She wanted the bloodline to continue. She wanted William to become a father.

Chapter Ten
William's Story

As long as he could remember, William had yearned for only one thing. Paternal love. He knew that no matter what he did for Mother, she wouldn't love him. She never had. At some time in his childhood, he stopped seeking her attention and learned to switch off his emotions. He even switched off from the external world. No school, no friends and, as he got older, no job. William had never worked. Instead, he lived in his mind, with mainly his thoughts and feelings for company. He did not see himself as psychopathic, yet he felt no remorse or empathy when he kidnapped and killed his victims. He experienced boredom, so furtively watching his victims fed the stimulation he craved.

Once Father ended up in the garden, his life had changed. He had vague memories of going to school, drawing pictures of ghosts and witches at Hallowe'en and the teacher displaying them on the wall. He could remember lining up for lunch; he loved the puddings and custard. He couldn't remember having any friends. He sat next to Ian Waterford but they had rarely spoken to each other. That was okay.

Only Father used to speak to him. His father used to cut him thick slices of bread and smother them in butter and strawberry jam when he was hungry. Mother used to cook stews, usually chicken or beef, but not very often and then they had to last for days. Father would pick him up and hug him. The only person to ever hug him.

He had no memories of being carried up to bed or being read a bedtime story. He used to take himself to bed. Even Christmas was just another day. He thought that might have been different if his father had lived.

At eighteen, he had met Tracey and had killed for the first time. She worked the streets at night. William would pick her up in his neighbour's white Ford Escort and drive her to a run-down trading estate. For £20, they had sex.

This went on for three weeks in the early hours of Saturday morning. On the fourth visit, he shared with the stoned Tracey how he felt about her; that he was falling for her. William had read the situation badly. A deep desire for affection and a relationship had become an obsession. He had started to put the drug-addicted painfully-thin Tracey, with her platinum-blonde wig, on a pedestal. In his world, she made him feel secure and he thought his feelings were reciprocated. She had laughed in his face and commented that if she had a pound for every time she'd heard that ...!

William had not expected her to laugh at him. He regarded the sex as a form of commitment. Rejection consumed him and it was followed by an intense irrational desire to kill.

He couldn't remember killing his platinum-blonde girlfriend. He just remembered a murderous mist of anger and squeezing her throat as he beat her head against the front window of the passenger seat. It was minutes later that he realised she had stopped moving, so he let go. Her body flopped against the passenger door.

Something in him flipped. He felt no remorse or guilt for her death. It was all her fault. He stretched over and opened the door. Her body tipped from the passenger seat headfirst. He started the car and began to drive. The rest of Tracey left the car. He only stopped to reach over again and close the car door. He never looked back or glanced in the mirror to see her body, lifeless and discarded on the ground.

No one came looking for him or came to arrest him after that night. Not that he cared if they did. She had deserved it. He did reflect on the night and decided that he wanted someone to live with him and his mother. Then they would grow to love him.

His mother thought it was a good idea but she said he had to choose carefully. They didn't want anyone causing them any trouble. Mother selected the first victim for them to murder together. She was called Grace. He used to watch her coming and going from the children's home. She was sixteen years old. Mother 'bumped' into her one day in the street, dropping the little shopping she had in her bag on the ground. Dark-haired plump Grace picked it up. Mother told her that she struggled to carry even the smallest amount and offered Grace money to carry it for her. It was so easy.

William was waiting upstairs at home for their return. Mother offered her a coffee, mixed with Ketamine and sleeping tablets. She stayed with them for four months. During her stay, Mother insisted he moved the shed to a new spot and dig another hole. She never used the word grave. William had wanted a child but Grace never got pregnant, so he had killed her by strangulation. Mother had watched. She was so happy with him that day.

There were so many victims that neither could remember all their names, but William vividly remembered what they looked like. Mostly blonde. He could, however, remember the names of his last two guests. Helen had stayed with them before Faith took her place.

79

Helen had left home at sixteen and went up north to be nearer Manchester where she had a small part in a theatre play. She was eighteen when the Grey Trench Coat Man met her. Mother had pretended to feel poorly and Helen helped her home. She was very quiet, compliant and aloof. She stayed nearly a year before Mother stabbed her, for fun. Just once, slowly in her heart, then they watched her die.

Before she came to stay, he had kept in the shadows watching her go to work or do her shopping. He even went to see her on stage at the local Theatre Royal, in a play called An Inspector Calls. She never knew he was watching her. He watched silently for three months, getting ready to trap her.

There were moments when he wished Mother hadn't killed her. He had liked having sex with her when she was asleep after drinking the special tea. The tea Mother made. At times, William went from feeling love to hate and rage for his mother. When she killed Helen, he hid the rage. He had loved her and now she was gone. No matter how much he hated his mother, he would never kill her. Even though at times she deserved it.

Things changed with Faith. Or maybe Faith changed William. He had watched her too, for a while, quietly from the shadows. He had watched as she went to work, went out for lunch and shopped. He would drive past her house in the early hours. She was different. He wanted her to know he was hunting her. He wanted her to see him. It became a game between the hunter and the hunted. It was her long blonde hair that had drawn him and the strong feelings of desire for her. Sometimes, she would look at him. That pleased him for then he knew she wanted a relationship.

Chapter Eleven

Imogen stood, momentarily rooted to the pavement. Her new fiancé lay motionless on the road. The driver who had run over Aidan's legs leapt from his BMW.

"I didn't see him; I didn't see him," was all the shocked middle-aged man could say.

Reality hit Imogen and a huge sob escaped her throat as she spoke.

"Aidan, Aidan."

Kneeling beside him, she cradled his bleeding head in her lap, not thinking she could do more damage. The BMW driver was pacing up and down with his head bent into his hands. The driver who had hit Aidan first was visibly shaking, talking frantically into his mobile phone. His red SEAT León was parked up near them.

Imogen was frantic. She had waited so long for this person who now lay motionless on the road.

"Please move out of the way, Madam. Do you know the victim?"

The instruction came from an unfamiliar voice.

Imogen stayed still, her gaze moving towards the stranger. Her body started to shake involuntarily.

This wasn't supposed to happen. We were supposed to be in bed by now, celebrating our engagement and drinking champagne.

"Madam, please move out of the way."

The same voice, but the request had changed to a demand.

Someone was gently helping her up and removing her from the scene. Another person took her place. It was the emergency services. She hadn't even noticed that an ambulance had arrived on the scene.

Is Aidan dead?

She had seen the impact and presumed the worse. She forced her eyes to look at a bloodied, unresponsive Aidan.

A blanket had been placed over him, but not his face. One of the ambulance crew was fitting a collar to his neck. Another was inserting a drip into his arm. He was alive; just. She wanted to touch him in case these were his last moments but she couldn't get near, with the crew skilfully working on him. The driver of the car was shaking his head, a look of helplessness about him while a policeman was taking his details.

Aidan was being carried into the awaiting ambulance. Forcing her legs to function, she followed in a daze and climbed in behind his stretcher.

"I'm his wife."

She aimed the statement at a paramedic who was holding up the drip attached to Aidan's arm. She knew her words weren't quite true. The truth was too painful, having to explain that she had been engaged for less than an hour. Seated next to Aidan in the ambulance, she finally took his hand in hers. A police officer, Sarah Jenkins, who had been trying to get her statement when she had gently removed her from Aidan, was sitting next to her. She was still talking, maybe with words of comfort. Imogen had zoned out. She began to weep and then huge sobs racked her body. Life was so unkind. Deep down, she knew there was no way he was going to survive this.

Instinct is a powerful force. Eleven minutes later, the ambulance arrived at the hospital. Aidan was dead. Imogen had lost her fiancé.

A young nurse, Sophie Blacklock, brought her a cup of coffee and she held the plastic cup firmly in her trembling hands. Her mind was cast back to the times they had shared. The good, the bad and all the hours she had spent waiting for him to ring. Sometimes he would make her wait for days. Then there were the arguments but none of them seemed important now. She just wanted him to have lived. What if he had survived but was paralysed? It didn't matter, she told herself, as long as he was alive. At least if he had ended up spending his remaining days in a wheelchair, they would have been able to marry. Their lives would have changed. She would have given up her job to care for him or worked freelance until he had adjusted.

Thoughts bounced around her head. She had desperately wanted Aidan to live, no matter at what cost. Staring at the diamond ring on her finger, it seemed even more precious than it had done an hour ago. It was the last thing he had given to her. She started to cry once more. Someone gently touched her shoulder. It was Sophie.

"The doctor will speak to you shortly."

Nodding through the torrent of tears, she watched as a stressed and tired-looking man in a green coat approached her. He looked to be in his early thirties, with dark hair and dark eyes, like Aidan. Imogen dropped her head to wipe her eyes and blow her nose.

"Mrs Handford. Hello, my name is Doctor Robinson."

Rising slowly, she shook the doctor's hand, wiping away the tears on her arm first.

"I'm his fiancée, not his wife. We were engaged tonight."

The words were too painful. Sobbing, she found herself clinging to the doctor; a total stranger. She was devastated. The doctor let her embrace him. Sadly, he'd dealt with this situation many times. The same scene, just different bereaved characters.

"Aidan had some very serious injuries," he continued as he gently broke their embrace. "His pelvis was fractured, he had broken his right arm and, unfortunately, he had internal damage and a fatal head injury. Would you like the hospital to contact his parents? Do you know their number?"

His parents? She had never really heard him talk about them. She knew he had an Aunt Dorothy who he was close to, but she didn't know her number.

"Sorry, I have never met his parents. Can I see him?"

There was hope in her voice.

Indicating with his arm for her to take a seat back in the side-waiting room, the doctor replied, "Please, wait here and I will arrange that for you."

She sat. The smell of antiseptic filled her nostrils. Tears streamed down her face. She felt that her heart had been physically broken; grief absorbed every cell of her body. Yet again, someone had stolen him away. They always did.

Doctor Robinson returned half an hour later to take her to see Aidan for the last time.

*

Three miles away, at 11.13 pm, Aunt Dorothy woke with a start. She could have sworn Aidan had been calling her name. For a second, she froze. She could see him standing next to her bed. Was she dreaming? He was smiling. He was smiling at her, and then he disappeared.

Turning on the bedside lamp, her heart pounded and she felt rattled. Worse still, she didn't think it had been a dream. It had been a premonition. She picked up the bedside phone and rang Aidan's number. His phone rang and rang. It was the fifth ring before a voice answered.

Chapter Twelve

William did not expect the judge to hand him a life sentence. Who was going to visit his mother? It was Faith's fault. It was her fault that he had to be separated from his mother. Anger burned within him.

He couldn't remember much about the day. He remembered seeing her in court, dressed in a plain black dress, playing the victim with her new darker hair colour. He found her hair unattractive. He wouldn't have followed her for months if it had been that colour.

There was a lot of media around the case. William was famous. The Grey Trench Coat Man was how the media had labelled him; a reference to his grey trilby hat and grey trench coat. Both had belonged to his father. Mother had never thrown his clothes out after his death, keeping up the pretence that he had run off with a younger woman and would come back one day. She had even told her son the same story.

He never told her that he knew she'd buried him. He had seen her. He had gone to the window as an innocent little boy. As he had turned away with tears running down his face, he knew his mother's wickedness was in him too. He could feel it.

He'd seen his father's bones when he dug in the same grave to bury Helen. It hadn't helped that the police had found his father and Helen buried in the garden. He could remember his legal team speaking to him briefly after sentencing. Tarquin Ludlow QC explained that he was going to have to serve at least fourteen years of the 17-year sentence before they could apply for parole. That he'd been lucky to get a sentence where parole was even possible. He would start his sentence in a Category A high-security prison; Belmarsh, in South-East London. A prison where only one man is believed to have escaped after blatantly walking through the prison gates posing as another inmate who was due for release.

William felt it would be a different world to HMP Frankland in County Durham, where he'd been on remand. He was right.

*

As William entered Britain's most secure prison, the atmosphere changed. It was austere. Security cameras monitored your every move, and prison officers gave off a 'Don't fuck with me' aura. He felt fear and humiliation. Those emotions had previously been foreign to him.

William was aware that a slim-built male officer with a shaved head, about thirty years old, was talking to him. He struggled to comprehend the words. His heart was beating too fast and there was a whooshing in his ears.

"You fucking deaf?"

The officer didn't look amused.

"I said, STRIP."

William remained silent. Fear was now being replaced by anger. There were four officers present. He carefully and slowly started to strip. He placed his grey trench coat and trilby on the table in front of him, and then he removed his dirty white shirt and grey trousers. He stood in threadbare socks, a washed-out white vest and baggy Y-fronts.

"You shy? And the rest. And hurry the fuck up."

The shaved-head officer now looked pissed off.

William removed his socks, then vest and finally his baggy underwear. He was completely naked. He covered his genitals with both hands, his skinny ashen body exposed.

"Open your mouth and stick out your tongue."

The shaved officer now looked bored. There was something about this prisoner that he found eery. The smell of body odour filled the room.

The instructions continued.

"Show me behind your ears. Spread your toes. Lift your feet, one at a time. Now squat, spread your butt checks and cough three times."

William hesitated for a moment, squatted over a mirror and coughed, as instructed. He pictured throttling the life out of the prison officer after he had gouged his eyes out. He desperately wanted to take back control. Belmarsh wouldn't break him. He was too dark and immoral. The challenge would be to get through his lengthy custodial sentence without committing murder. It was a yearning that was extremely hard to crush.

After a night on the medical block to check he wasn't suicidal, William was moved to the Induction Block. He became a prisoner with ID number DH819733.

The cell walls had been painted a shade of green. Not light or dark, but somewhere in between. It was small with a bed, toilet, chair and table; all smaller than he was used to. If he sat on the chair, his spindly legs could easily touch the bed. The confined space measured nine feet by six. The bed had a thin pillow, sheet and green blanket which reminded William of home. Mother always insisted on sheets and blankets although, in prison, the sheets were cleaner.

He also had a kettle. An officer had explained that he was entitled to a small allowance where he could buy snacks and drinks from the canteen shop. Prison life would soon teach him how much you could barter for with a tin of tuna or packet of Digestives. He hated the Induction Block. It was nicknamed Beirut as it was like a war zone with angry dangerous men about to start a lengthy prison sentence, with time on their hands and nothing to lose. William avoided showering and kept his head down in the exercise yard as those were the areas where scores were settled and blood was shed.

After a few weeks, he was moved onto a permanent wing in one of the four house blocks. He later learnt that Belmarsh was designed to minimise the risk of escape and violence and any of the four house blocks could easily be shut down in an emergency.

He hated the noise. The constant banging of metal on metal, prisoners bellowing throughout the night and loud music. He wasn't a fan of the music. Mother always listened to BBC Radio 4.

His block was for lifers. After serving anywhere between ten and thirty years of their sentence, they could be considered for parole. Most wanted to stay out of trouble and do their time, hoping for at least a downgrade to Category B or C for good behaviour.

For the first few weeks, William had a single cell. He was pleased and relieved he didn't have to share with a murderer, rapist, terrorist or drug dealer. He saw himself as different.

He wasn't a criminal; Faith was. She'd tried to burn him and his mother to death. He wasn't a religious man but, to survive, he had to have faith in himself. The irony was not lost on him, as wanting to have Faith had led to incarceration, for a very long time. The isolation was intolerable, even with a TV, although he only felt safe when he was locked in his cell. The world of violence, gangs and drugs was unfamiliar to him. He was familiar with some drugs although he'd never used them. Instead, he had used them on his victims to keep them quiet and submit to his yearnings. He was familiar with the effects of Ketamine. Here, Heroin was widely used and available.

At 9 am, he'd be let out to the exercise yard. He hated walking around and around, avoiding eye contact and rarely speaking to the other inmates. Others walked around and around for forty-five minutes, while some stood in small groups.

Then he'd be locked up again until teatime. Some inmates were let out for longer if they had jobs or scheduled visits. No one visited William.

There was also the Association Room where inmates played pool, table tennis or cards, known as the Spur. He'd never experienced any of those games so he avoided them. Instead, he would sit and stare at the TV.

He didn't trust anyone. Most of the inmates knew why he was there, thanks to the media coverage. He lived in fear of his true crimes being exposed. The other girls he'd disposed of over the years, without feelings or remorse.

Every day started the same way. He'd eat breakfast sitting on his bed. This was provided the night before in a plastic bag when inmates went for their last meal of the day. The bag contained breakfast cereal, milk, a teabag, sugar and jam. He'd boil the small kettle and make himself the only cup of tea he had during the day. Later he was told if there was any trouble, the electricity would be switched off before officers entered any cells, or 'rooms' as they called them.

This was explained to him one day by Freddie in the Association Room.

Chapter Thirteen

At the age fifty-five, Elizabeth Channing was sent to HMP Low Newton, Brasside in County Durham. It served courts from the Scottish Borders to Cumbria and North Yorkshire. It held 219 prisoners. Enduring the uncomfortable journey in a prison van, known as the sweat box, she could see out but was told no one could see in. This was beneficial as the media were, in her opinion, intrusive and disrespectful.

Getting checked into prison was slow, with so many forms to complete, and humiliating. After what seemed like hours of waiting in a holding cell and a rub-down strip search, she was shown to a small private room by two female officers. There the degrading experience peaked. Elizabeth had always been in control. All that control was stripped from her and it was an experience she did want to have again. She wanted to slowly kill everyone in the room. Her body and face might have aged badly but the darkness within her had intensified.

"Right, Channing," said one of the officers, "I'm Hazel Kay and this is Sue Henry. We need to do another strip search and then ask you to sit in that special chair."

Elizabeth froze. She was the one who liked to make people feel uncomfortable. To see them vulnerable or hurting. She learned that the special chair was called a B.O.S.S. chair. Body Orifice Security Scanner. It was grey and black and looked more like a large step with a backrest. Sue Henry explained it had non-intrusive sensors designed to detect small weapons or contraband concealed in the abdominal cavity, rectum, vagina and nasal cavities. Kay and Henry didn't look like they were enjoying the experience either. First, Elizabeth removed her blue polyester dress, washed-out bra, American tan tights and washed-out knickers.

"Put your arms above your head and turn around," instructed Kay. "Do you need support to lift your feet?"

Elizabeth ignored her question and lifted one foot slowly and gently, replacing it slowly to regain her balance before lifting the other. Her underwear and dress were returned but not her tights. Putting her dress on, she then sat on the special chair.

After the search, there were more questions before going back to a holding cell. She had been offered one phone call. She declined. She had no one to call as William was also serving time.

More time passed. Then questions again from the medical staff. No, she wasn't suicidal. No, not alcohol dependent. No, never touched drugs. After the medical, Elizabeth was handed an identity card which she was informed she had to always carry. It had a photo of an old tired-looking woman. With sadness, she realised it was her. Time had not been kind. It also said Elizabeth Channing, DOB 10.07.1949 and prison number MN10792.

Then there were more forms. She didn't admit she couldn't read very well. Even William didn't know. She had newspapers piled up at home, which she had pretended to read for years. She could mostly work out from the photos what was going on. She signed the various forms, having no idea what they were. The downside of hardly ever attending school.

She accepted the various leaflets which were apparently about life at HMP Low Newton and the support available. Then she was escorted through numerous locked gates towards the Psychologically Informed Planned Environment (PIPE) wing, known as the I-Wing. At her trial, her defence lawyer had put it to the jury that Elizabeth Channing was likely suffering from a personality disorder which went back to her unstable childhood. An independent psychologist testified this could be probable and that she suffered from Avoidant Personality Disorder.

Inmates were not treated for their disorders on PIPE. Instead, it was designed as a supportive environment to promote the development of prisoners by specially trained officers who would facilitate their progression. Elizabeth felt she was surrounded by nutcases. Some of them had committed sexual offences against children but the maximum it could house was thirty-nine people. At that point, it held twenty-five. Better than some of the other wings.

Elizabeth had a cell of her own. Next door, her cellmate was Mandy Croft, known as Oddcroft on the wing because of her peculiar behaviour. Now in her seventies, she had spent her adult life back and forth between short bursts of freedom and prison. In her early twenties, she was first imprisoned for shoplifting after her fourth time in front of the judge. She stole to feed herself and buy alcohol. Then she began to steal to order. She didn't care when she got caught. If she wanted it, she took it.

Now she was serving another four years for theft and GBH. She had attacked the security guard who detained her and then the policeman who arrested her. Not that she could remember as it was all a drunken blur. She had stolen, all her life. It was all she knew. She was estranged from her family and never had any friends. If she didn't steal alcohol, she had other goods to sell to her neighbours so that she could buy alcohol. She had also been labelled by the medical profession as Schizotypal.

She sat on her bunk of the small cell, looking at the old pallid woman who had stopped at her cell door, clutching a plastic bag with her few belongings. She didn't know what had happened in that stranger's life for her to commit such immoral crimes, but their paths had now crossed, and they had one thing in common. To spend their final years banged up.

Elizabeth nodded at the white-haired petite woman who stared from the neatly-made bunk. Tucking her short white bob behind her ear, Mandy slowly rose and stood. At 4ft 10in, she was barely any taller than when she was sitting. She wore bright pink leggings and a purple sweatshirt. Part of her disorder made Oddcroft paranoid and distrustful of others. She wanted to see what exactly was in the stranger's plastic bag.

"Shall I help you make the bed?"

Oddcroft knew who the old woman was, standing before her. It had been all over the news. This was the woman who lured a young girl for the **Grey Trench Coat Man**, although she hadn't been charged with that offence.

"Thank you," said Elizabeth.

She handed over the two sheets and green blanket she'd been given after the endless forms were completed. As Oddcroft stretched her arms to take the bedding, Elizabeth saw the red scars running across her arms. Something she did occasionally to help release the anxiety which consumed her.

She'd never been a self-harmer until she came to prison. Elizabeth, being Elizabeth, started to think about how she could use this vulnerable woman to her advantage. Maybe the next few years inside wouldn't be too bad.

Chapter Fourteen

Dot turned off the local news. The images of her older sister and nephew disappeared from the screen. The reporter had a dreary face with a voice to match as he recounted some of the key points of the trial. Fifty-six-year-old Elizabeth Channing, mother of thirty-four-year-old William Channing who was dubbed the Grey Trench Coat Man, was today jailed for six years for the manslaughter of her husband, Alfred Channing.

Dot could not remember how many years had passed since she'd seen or spoken to her sister. She thought about the loss she had experienced in her own life. She was widowed young, lost her niece Abbey Winter to cancer, and hadn't spoken to Abbey's mother, her younger sister Natalie, since the spectacle at the funeral. Her dear nephew, Aidan Handford, had also been taken far too young at thirty-five, in a road accident. Her mind went back to the phone call she'd made to his mobile and the dread she felt when a female voice answered. It belonged to his bereaved fiancée, Imogen Fernsby, informing her that Aidan had been killed. Life could be so cruel.

Imogen left journalism after his death and wrote and published her first children's book, called Biscuit and the Snail. It was about a hamster named Biscuit and his best friend, Snail, who went on garden adventures. She had dedicated it to Aidan.

Dorothy's family was getting smaller and now two members were in prison. She wondered what her life would have been like if she hadn't moved into the stable caring home of her grandparents. Her parents weren't bad people but they were selfish. Only had time for each other and having a good time. No routine family life for them. Both parents had died years ago. Her father from a heart attack and her mother had caught the flu which turned into bronchitis. She hadn't been close to them.

Now Elizabeth had been sentenced to six years and William was serving seventeen.

Dot had many friends in the community. She met her friends, Mabel and Janice, every Wednesday for Bingo, did a food shop on a Thursday and helped out in her local church, usually arranging the flowers. But the loss she felt was deep. She felt lonely. She felt guilty. She felt ashamed.

The secret she had carried for over thirty years was consuming her. She was no better than her elder sister. There was only one thing to do.

Visit Elizabeth.

Chapter Fifteen

William was on his usual seat, staring at but not really watching the television. A documentary about the sea and the impact of plastics.

"It's fifteen years since I've seen the sea."

The voice, William was about to learn, was Freddie's. He was thirty-five years of age and made a lot of use of the prison gym. His muscular arms were decorated with faded tattoos.

William glanced his way and gave a nod to show he had at least heard the mass of the man.

"I know who you are," continued Freddie. "The Grey Trench Coat Man. Can I call you Grey?"

"My name is William."

His voice sounded unfamiliar to him, as he rarely spoke.

Freddie laughed, "Okay, William. How are you finding it here?"

"I find being locked up, for some days for 23 hours a day, infuriating."

William surprised himself with his response, but it was true.

"You need to get a job. It gets you out of the cell more and you get paid. You can order stuff then, like chocolate, cigarettes and biscuits," Freddie said helpfully.

As William started to process how he felt about more time out of confinement at the cost of having to be around delinquents, he learned why the electricity was switched off at times in the cells.

A man walked in front of the TV. He slowed his pace to look at someone that William hoped was sitting behind him. Or was he staring at him? His face was an angry red from the nose down, his skin potholed, and you could see where some of his skin had fallen away. Nasty scabs had formed where the injury was starting to heel. It looked like black stains on raw steak.

He stood, momentarily watching the inmates watch him. Then, slowly, he moved on.

"That's Tyler," muttered Freddie. "He's in for armed robbery but owed Owen Flinch, Flinn as we call him, two packets of smokes. So, he and his gang jugged him."

William looked at Freddie with confusion on his face but didn't speak.

Freddie continued, "They put sugar in the kettle and boiled it. Then threw it in his face. It makes the burns worse. His skin bubbled up and then tore clean away. It was a warning to pay up. Next time, they'll pour it down his throat. That's why the screws turn the electricity off in our cells if there's trouble, then wait before they come in. So we don't do it to them."

"Why was he staring?"

William hoped it wasn't at him. He'd never had to strangle a man before but he'd give it a go if he had to. The thought pleased him.

"McKenzie is behind us. One of Flinch's gang, who probably helped with the punishment. Keep your head down around them and don't ask them for any favours as you'll be expected to repay double. There are about two hundred different gangs here. You can get shanked by just living in the wrong postcode. Stick with me and I'll look out for you."

William studied the bulk of the man next to him. He seemed friendly, contrary to his appearance. Maybe this could be his first-ever friendship.

"How long have you been here?" he asked.

"Three years. Got another nineteen years to serve. They'll probably move me somewhere else soon. They do that with lifers. Move us from cell to cell regularly and another prison after a few years."

Freddie said the words as if twenty-two years were weeks. He had accepted that freedom was a long way off.

William hesitated before asking the next question as this man had a longer sentence than him.

"What did you do?"

The look in Freddie's eyes changed. He looked eerily excited.

"Come on, William. Someone should have told you that we don't talk about that. But seeing as you asked, I'll tell you what I've allegedly done. I was charged with murder. Same as you, Mr Grey Trench Coat Man."

William ignored the media label.

"Murder? Then why so long?"

At that moment, William felt superior that no one knew of the years of killing he had committed. Otherwise, he would never be freed.

"I allegedly slit a woman's throat," said Freddie, shrugging his shoulders at the same time.

What William would learn during his time in prison was that no one is honest about their crimes. They gave their version. What Frederick 'Freddie' Landa had done to receive such a long stay in Her Majesty's Prison Service was true. He had slit the throat of a woman. Three times. Three victims whose throats he had sliced because he had the urge to.

The first victim was only seventeen years old. He'd met her while they were running in the park. A week later he killed her. The second victim was a year later. A year when he had waited for the police to come kicking in his door. Nothing. He felt confident. The same method was used on thirty-two-year-old Stacie Samms but it was a different park. The third victim was in her own home. He'd seen the fifty-year-old admiring herself in the gym. She had irritated him. After a couple of weeks of watching Beatrice Pashley, and secretly following the divorcee on various social media sites, he had followed her home. She had ferociously fought back. Not only did he slit her throat, but he also sliced her open from her stomach to her breastbone. He'd left his DNA and was seen entering her property, and identified in a line-up, by a neighbour.

A bell rang and a grumble went up from the Association Room. Their hour was up. Time for the inmates to be locked behind the heavy metal doors of their cells again. William was pleased. He also vowed not to get into many conversations for the rest of his long sentence.

As the men shuffled forward, he heard a yell and then someone roughly pushed past him. He wasn't sure what had happened. There were officers, or screws as everyone called them, yelling to get back into their cells. Tyler was being restrained on the floor with his arms pulled up his back. Turning around, William saw McKenzie lying on his side, clutching his stomach. Blood spread across his white T-shirt. He'd been shanked. The crude weapon lay on the floor. It had originally been one side of a pair of scissors, about six inches long, sharpened on both sides and then wrapped in masking tape. William wondered how he'd managed to conceal it. Before they entered any room, they underwent a body search.

"Bang goes his parole," said Freddie as they passed Tyler, still pinned to the floor.

That day, William was pleased to be confined to his cell. He wondered whom to ask for some paper so he could write to his mother. Up until that moment, he had not crossed paths with his next victim, Daryl Sinnatt. Officer Sinnatt, to give him his work title.

Some officers showed prisoners respect and got the same back, and some exploited their power and were nasty. Daryl was nasty and William was going to experience just how much.

Chapter Sixteen

Elizabeth loathed prison life and despised the staff and inmates. Every day she wore the same grey prison-issued tracksuit bottoms and sweatshirt. She was better than everyone around her. She did not want to wear similar clothes to them. You could buy clothes from the prison's shop Rags to Riches or they had second-hand clothes from which you could pick. She had refused both. She'd didn't need any extra clothes. She would put her dress back on, the day she was released. She would be released. She refused to die without seeing William again.

Every day was the same. Noisy and structured. You would imagine the PIPE wing to be quiet because of the small numbers. Far from it.

Originally from Birmingham, fifty-six-year-old Google ran the wing. Nicknamed Google because there was nothing she didn't know about prison life or what the gossip (there was always gossip) was on the wing.

One morning, Elizabeth was woken by Google hitting her chair continuously on her cell door as it was her granddaughter's birthday and she wanted to phone her to wish her a happy birthday before school.

Regarding her personal safety, Elizabeth felt reasonably safe when she was outside her cell. No one asked her outright what her crime was. Officers were more likely to be assaulted by a prisoner than she was.

Most days were spent in her cell. Breakfast was given to her the night before and was eaten at the small table. There was also a small wardrobe, a set of drawers on which a TV stood, and a chair. All cells had a toilet and her wing and F-wing had in-cell showers. F-Wing was home to women who had long-term and indeterminate sentences, restricted status or those who were part of the Primrose Unit which provided specialist treatment for high-risk offenders. Elizabeth had heard stories of killer Rose West serving her time on F-Wing by baking cakes and knitting. She had to be moved when another inmate threatened to kill her.

Lunch was a hot meal served at noon, when they were also given a packed meal for their tea. If they were short-staffed, it was as early as 11 am. There was a reading group that Elizabeth sometimes went along to, just to listen to the other inmates. She pretended she couldn't read the books because of her poor eyesight. This helped cover the fact she didn't know how to. Her day also included queuing up twice for her angina medication.

Sometimes she would go along to see the chaplain on a Sunday with a small group of the other misfits, as she saw them. She wasn't a religious woman, but it got her out of the cell and she found the services and chats interesting. It also helped her to pick out the vulnerable women.

There was only one person in the prison who made her feel uncomfortable. She did not like being in that woman's presence. She was not an inmate, but a member of staff. Psychologist Dr Angelica Gallo was born to an English mother and an Italian father. She was an expert in the field of personality disorders and had joined HMP Low Newton eight months previously. She was in her mid-forties and didn't wear a wedding ring or any other jewellery. Her dark hair was cut in a trendy short pixie style and her toned body was always covered by black trousers and a formal blouse. Her look was finished with barely-there makeup.

At their first meeting, her brown eyes never left Elizabeth's face. She studied her every move and listened intently to every word she spoke, interpreting each jerk of the foot, each shrug of the shoulder and each slow blink of her eyes.

Their next meeting would be in three days. That bothered Elizabeth. She was mulling over how to get out of it when Officer Lee appeared with photocopies of the Wing's letters. Parcels for those sentenced had been suspended to help control drug smuggling. Personal letters were photocopied and then handed out. The originals were held back as some inmates had been receiving theirs laced with Class A drugs.

"Channing, you have a visitor's request."

Officer Lee appeared at the doorway of her cell. He was 6ft 2in, with a shaven head and was in his mid-thirties. The women liked him. He showed them respect.

Rising from the small table, where she had been doing a jigsaw puzzle of a white cottage with a black Labrador lying in a garden with various bright flowers, her heart rate increased. Could William somehow have been released? Opening the photocopy, she recognised the name immediately. Dorothy Heist. Her sister. After all these years, what did she want?

With time on her hands, she decided to accept the visitation and find out.

Chapter Seventeen

The familiar sound of the key releasing the heavy lock woke William.

"Get up. Shower time."

Officer Sinnatt's voice irritated William's ears. It sounded more like a command than a statement.

Freddie shot out of the room carrying his towel, bar of soap and shampoo. He'd been sat ready to be one of the first in the showers that morning while they were relatively clean and didn't smell of piss.

William had not showered since he'd arrived. He'd heard stories of the brutality that occurred in the showers when the guards were outside. It was a suitable time to settle scores. Shanks, heavy objects in socks, and beatings. He'd kept away. There was a small sink in the room and, when he did wash, he used that.

He liked the unkempt look. It hid more of his face. He'd rarely shaved on the outside and didn't see the point now. Mother used to cut his hair. Never once had he been to the barbers, and he didn't intend to visit the one in the prison.

Getting up out of his narrow bed, he used the toilet. Then, without washing his hands, he sat at the small table to have his small box of cereal with UHT milk which he'd collected the night before at mealtime.

He wondered if he should sign up to use the exercise yard. He missed the thrill of just standing, watching people. It thrilled him when they knew they were being watched. The inmates so far had left him alone. They thought he was weird.

Freddie entered the cell, interrupting William's thoughts.

"You not showering?"

Freddie's nose wrinkled as he spoke.

"You are starting to whiff a bit if you don't mind me saying."

William slowly turned his head, trying hard to keep all emotion from his face.

Why did Freddie say that? I thought we were beginning to be friends. I wonder how long it would take to strangle someone with a tourniquet made from a bed sheet?

He held that thought.

Officer Slug, known to others as Office Sinnatt, was at the doorway. His round face, and even rounder stomach, reminded William of a slug. He'd happily squash him. Since being banged up he found his thoughts had turned darker. He couldn't physically kill him as he'd lose his chance of parole. Instead, he fantasised in painstaking detail about what he would do when he could kill him without having to pay the price. He did, after all, have a track record of undiscovered murders.

William was classed as a standard prisoner but, if he attacked an officer, he would be downgraded to basic. Fewer privileges. If he was enhanced, there were areas of the prison he could enter which had more space, comfortable chairs and a pool table. William was happy to stay under the radar as standard. To become enhanced, he would have to be a trained Listener, when he would listen to other prisoners' concerns, be a cleaner or work in the kitchens.

"Channing, you have an appointment with Dr Archer. Follow me."

Again, Slug said the words as a command.

"No one told me."

"You refusing an officer's request? Do you want to be put on a report?"

What is Slug's problem?

William had been raised to hate authority. Mother was right. They were all corrupt. Slowly shaking his head to confirm to Slug that he did not want to be put on a report (as he was always thinking about parole or even early release), he followed him, wearing the same shirt and trousers he'd slept in. Sixteen hours had passed since he'd been allowed out of his cell. At least, he could stretch his legs. Often, they'd be locked up from 5 pm until the next morning.

Escorted by Officer Sinnatt, William walked along the long corridors, waiting while gates were opened and then locked securely behind them. The noise was deafening. Chatter from the men, and music that William didn't recognise, boomed from different cells. Freddie had a radio. It was the first time he had heard Radio 1. Mother always listened to Radio 4.

They stopped at a door in the vicinity of the cell block. The door plaque read 'Dr Andreas Archer'. William presumed it was the doctor's name as he couldn't read very well. Mother had never taught him.

"Hello, William. It's good to see you again. Come in and take a seat. Thank you, Officer," said Andreas, as he rose from his desk to close the door, leaving Officer Sennit outside. He was the only member of staff who called inmates by their Christian names. He said it was important for them to feel at ease with him. It helped to build rapport in the psychologist/patient relationship.

Dr Andreas Archer was known as the Shrink. In his early thirties, he'd been a psychologist at HMP Belmarsh for five years. Freddie had already told William to play along as it would go in his favour with the parole board. It was their second meeting.

The office was sparse. It had dark grey comfortable chairs and a small table with a box of tissues. The doctor's desk and chair were in the corner. On the wall, there were three colour paintings. Of nothing, just colourful swirls. The vibrant colours looked out of place in such a bland setting.

Andreas' appearance was the opposite of William's. He was well-groomed with dark floppy hair and dark-framed glasses. He wore jeans (William always wore grey trousers) and a blue and grey checked lumberjack-style shirt. He was a nice person and treated all the inmates and officers with respect.

"How are you settling in?"

The doctor's hazel eyes watched William as he took a seat opposite him. He ignored the stale stench of body sweat. He wasn't the first inmate he'd profiled who wasn't showering regularly, if at all.

"I'm fine."

William was always a man of few words. He could feel his heartbeat rising. He didn't want to be with the nice shrink who might uncover his secrets. He pushed the images of some of his victims from his mind. It excited him too much.

"Last time, we discussed your childhood and your father not being in your life from such a young age. Today, I'd like you to tell me about your mother. How would you describe your relationship?"

Silence filled the room.

The doctor waited calmly for William to reply. The silence continued. William felt very uncomfortable. He thought carefully about his words, choosing those he thought the doctor wanted to hear.

"She is a good mother. Until recently, she has never left me."

The thought of separation from his mother made his stomach churn in slow, painful knots.

"Yes, your mother is in Low Newton women's prison. How does that make you feel?"

The doctor's biro poised, waiting for the response, while his eyes searched William's pale harrowed face.

"Mother doesn't deserve to be inside. She didn't do anything wrong."

He said the words slowly and controlled.

The doctor was used to hearing denial. Probably fifty per cent of lifers would say they were innocent and that the police had stitched them up because they were known to them, and it made their jobs easier.

Andreas glanced down at his notes, for show. He knew Prisoner DH819733 William Channing's notes in detail. They were ingrained in his memory. After their first meeting, he had felt there was much more to this smooth-talking controlled, yet insincere, man. Experience had taught him that the lack of empathy, remorse and guilt present in William meant that he was sitting opposite a very dangerous man. He also knew the crimes he'd been recently incarcerated for; the ones they knew about. It was extremely likely that there were many more.

"Who do you think buried your father in the garden?"

"Not Mother!"

William snapped the response back. His emotional composure was cracking. Andreas said nothing. He was comfortable with silence. He waited and watched.

William kept his body and hands still. He knew he was being watched. Being judged. He had to win this doctor over, so he changed tack. Picturing his mother in prison, surrounded by murderers, drug takers and thieves, he willed tears to his eyes. Blinking to enable the false tears to fall onto his cheeks, he made his next calculated move.

Breathing deeply to add to the effect, he slightly lowered his head and deliberately raised his shoulders, hoping to give the impression of a man experiencing grief.

"It wasn't Mother's fault. I can remember that day. I was about four years old. I remember the raised voices. Mother was screaming. Father was yelling. I was scared. I climbed out of bed and crept down the creaky stairs. The stairs and landing were in darkness. The house was cold and the kitchen door was open. Light shone through. I peeked through the door. Father had Mother by the throat. I couldn't move. I saw Mother's hand reach for the knife on the kitchen bench."

William shook his head, pretending to shake the shocking image out of it.

"I saw her grab the knife. That's when I saw Father fall to the floor with a loud thump. She had to. Otherwise, he would have killed her. He'd met someone else and was going to leave us."

William wiped his eyes and nose on his shirt sleeves to hide the smirk spreading across his face. He knew it was a lie. He could remember that night. He remembered Mother screaming at Father who was trying to calm her down. Then she picked up the knife and stabbed him over and over, even when he lay dead on the floor.

He would always protect her. He just wanted her to love him. Even when she wanted him to kill young girls. He enjoyed killing. It had pleased Mother as she had enjoyed watching him.

Andreas waited until the performance was over before glancing at his notepad to bullet-point what he'd witnessed.

- *Shallow emotions*
- *Lack of responsibility*
- *Is this the result of the Avoidant Attachment theory?*

He would write a full report after the session.

William was starting to enjoy himself, creating stories for the Shrink to analyse. He had the upper hand in their relationship since he had something this caring, smiling doctor did not have. Deceit.

"Have you ever been in love, William?"

The doctor caught a flicker of hurt in the damaged man's face. He doubted that William had ever experienced emotional intimacy. The painful sting of rejection drove him to kill. Even his mother didn't love him. She'd taught him manipulation, deceit and a lack of responsibility. They were the only behaviours he knew.

"I love Mother," came William's reply. "She is all I need."

"How are you finding the other inmates?"

The doctor again studied William's gaunt face as he flinched at the question. He didn't like anyone here. He hated the prison officers even more. Dictating when he went to bed, when he got up and when he could go outside. He especially hated Daryl Sinnatt. The officer had, for some reason, taken a dislike to him. William had already started to fantasise about killing him. He always shoved William roughly to go faster when he had to escort him anywhere and called him derogatory names. 'Putrid bastard' was a favourite.

"So far, they are okay."

The doctor waited for him to elaborate. Silence stretched out between them.

"Have you formed any friendships?"

The doctor knew that this would be extremely unlikely.

"Haven't been here long enough. Spend most of my day in the cell."

William was wondering where the question was leading.

"How are you finding your cellmate?"

William felt irritation bubble up inside because of the intrusive questions. He wanted to grab the doctor by the throat and smash his head against the wall. He wanted to stop the noise. He wanted to stop this trap.

The questions kept on coming. He didn't know how he was going to serve his time without committing murder. In the past, when his victims annoyed him, he would have happily killed them and then bury them in either his or next-door's garden. No one had lived next door for years.

He looked at the doctor and wondered if the prison had a garden.

Chapter Eighteen

Dot was nervous. She was off to visit her sister. A convicted murderer. She'd bought her some crisps, chocolate bars and bottled water. She hoped she would be allowed to pass them on.

She'd dressed her plump figure carefully for the occasion. A navy A-line dress, cream cardigan and flat navy shoes. She had filled up her Volkswagen Polo with petrol the night before and had prepared sandwiches in case she became hungry. The drive would take about forty minutes and she hoped she wouldn't get lost after the A167.

As it was, it was well-signposted. She thought it was odd that there were residential houses not too far from the prison. As well as a women's prison, part of it was a young offenders' institute and the sign for HM Prison and YOI Low Newton let her know she was in the right place. She pulled up into the large car park.

She felt guilty and blessed that her secret had not been exposed and never would be. She had to live with the guilt. She'd paid her penance in her own way. She'd given her life to society and cared for others. She had raised her niece, before cancer snatched her away, and she volunteered every week in her local church.

The queue ahead was long. She joined it and waited in silence, wondering who the people were going to see. What was their story? Some of them looked like they were ex-offenders as aggression and front radiated from them. Others were men, holding onto the hands of children, waiting to reunite them with their mothers.

"Come forward. Name?"

Dot answered. The officer who addressed her looked bored.

"Put your bag on there, then put it and your mobile phone in the locker."

Dot put her bag on what could only be described as a conveyor belt you see going through security at an airport. Or Windsor Castle. She remembered visiting there one summer when she had to put her bag on the security conveyor belt. Only the staff there were pleasant and smiley.

"I've got my sister some snacks. Can I give them to her?"

"They'll need to be checked first."

Empty-handed, Dot was escorted with some other visitors along corridors and a courtyard. Gates opened and shut. They couldn't get very far until they came to another locked gate. She was told her table number and she sat down. The room had several plastic tables and chairs.

She waited. Her heart was racing and her hands were clammy. Nerves consumed her. The noise levels increased and prisoners started to file in.

She recognised her sister from the media coverage. Her skinny long body was covered by a grey tracksuit.

Dot rose to her feet.

Am I allowed to embrace her?

Elizabeth stopped for a second before taking a seat, folding her arms purposely across her chest. The two women faced each other. Bonded by blood alone. Emotionally they were strangers.

"What do you want?"

Elizabeth's words were emotionless.

It wasn't what Dot had pictured. She thought her sister would have been pleased to see her. Pleased to have someone on the outside to visit her; to bring her magazines and snacks. Instead, an impersonal unsmiling ice queen sat before her.

"I have read your story in the papers and I wanted to make sure you were okay. Can I get you anything? I've brought you a few things which hopefully they will give you later."

Dot gave her sister a little smile.

Anger filled every part of Elizabeth's body.

"You have never been there for me," hissed Elizabeth. "You left me to live with our grandparents. I was left with no one. You had the life I should have had. Instead, I'm in here. Trapped."

"I'm sorry, Elizabeth. I was only a child. I thought you were happy on your own. You hardly ever spoke to me. Did you know Natalie had a child, but she has passed of cancer? She was called Abbey and was only twenty-nine."

Dot had desperately wanted the visit to go well. Maybe talking about family stuff would help.

"I never want to see you again. You are nothing to me."

Elizabeth's words were cold and flat. Dot couldn't understand such venom.

"Elizabeth, I'm leaving. Just remember that you are in here because you committed a murder. You stabbed your poor husband to death."

Dot started to push her chair back to leave when Elizabeth spoke.

"You are wrong. I didn't commit a murder. I've committed four!"

Elizabeth roared with laughter at the look of shock on Dot's face. She liked to make people feel uncomfortable. She remembered how good she felt when she had poisoned her husband's parents. She hadn't liked how close they were to their only son. Then there was Helen Boleyn; a sickly creature. She didn't feel any remorse that her son had taken the blame and was now serving the time.

*

Back in the safety of her car, Dot held onto the steering wheel. She hadn't even started the engine. She just needed something to hold. Her sister was evil.

But was she really any different to her sister?

She allowed the memory she had suppressed to come slowly into her mind. She had loved her husband, Richard. He had only been thirty-one when he passed. Two years before, he'd been diagnosed with pancreatic cancer. Six months before that, he'd started an affair with Annie Larson, the barmaid at their local. She was a similar age and had been widowed after she and her husband had been in a car accident. He had died instantly and their 6-month-old son died one week later. Left bereft and heading for financial ruin, she started work in the White Swan, the same one Elizabeth and Alfred had held their small wedding reception. The angry scars on her face and arms were a constant reminder of that life-shattering day. She had been wearing a seatbelt but her husband had not. For Richard, it was love at first sight. He hadn't seen the scars; he had seen a fighter.

Over the months, they grew close. They took their time. Annie was still drowning in grief and Richard was married. They had just started talking about a future together when his diagnosis came. He felt it was punishment for his betrayal.

Dot had gone into the mother-hen mode, making him great meals and taking him for his chemotherapy. However, after another gruelling session, his doctor explained that his survival rate past three years was less than ten per cent.

He wanted to spend his remaining years with Annie.

That night at home, he went upstairs in the smart tidy home he shared with Dot. She was lying on the bed with one of her headaches. He felt so weak and tired and, in any other circumstances, he would have joined her. Instead, he sat on the bed and said that he was truly sorry. He didn't want to spend his remaining years married to her. He had fallen in love.

Dot couldn't remember much of the argument. She couldn't remember the heated words they had exchanged. She just remembered how he had made her feel. Devasted, betrayed and worthless.

She remembered him saying that he was leaving and that he'd be back the next day for his things. In those last three minutes, her life had cruelly changed. He was her husband. She was not going to let him go.

She'd followed him out of the bedroom. He was slowly making his way downstairs, pale and frail from the powerful chemicals that had been pumped into his body to fight cancer. She knew what she was going to do. She pushed him with all her might. He fell headfirst, hitting the bottom of the stairs with a thud and his head impacted against the porch wall.

The memories of his lifeless body were still vivid. She had rung the paramedics and stuck as close to the truth as possible. They had been chatting in the bedroom. He went to go downstairs. He was weak from the treatment. She heard him fall and found him lifeless at the bottom of the stairs. No one doubted her story.

She had him cremated ten days later. She had seen her, Annie, at the back of the church. It was her fault. She had tried to take her husband.

Dot was a murderer. Was she really any different to Elizabeth? No, she just hadn't been caught and never would be.

Her secret would die with her.

Chapter Nineteen

The room was small. There was a desk and chair near the barred window which housed a laptop and a coffee cup. There were no personal photographs on display. In the other half of the room stood two green comfortable chairs with a small coffee table between them. A box of man-sized tissues had been deliberately placed on top.

I won't be needing those.

Elizabeth had been sitting in one of the comfortable chairs for only a few minutes. She had paid very little attention to the psychologist sitting opposite. She was small, in her late thirties and chubby. She had cropped black hair and an annoying chirpy voice. She looked more masculine than feminine.

Dr Angelica Gallo had worked for the Primrose Project for two years. It delivered an intervention programme for those inmates with dangerous or severe personality disorders. Her role was to offer psychological interventions to meet the individual needs of the prisoners, hoping that they would reduce the risk posed to others and themselves. The programme could cater for up to twelve inmates. Elizabeth Channing was number nine.

Angelica sat watching the woman before her, with arms folded defiantly across the grey sweatshirt and legs dressed in grey tracksuit bottoms crossed over at the knees, facing towards the door. It was clear that Elizabeth Channing was not going to make their second meeting easy. She kept her voice light, deliberately trying to win over the gaunt, angry woman.

"How are you?"

Elizabeth slowly turned her head to look into the face of the psychologist. The other inmates had warned her how the sessions went and that how much she gave them would impact her prospect of any future parole.

"Can I go back to my cell?"

Angelica glanced at the impersonal aloof prisoner before her.

"You can, at the end of the session. This is for your benefit. Last time we spoke about your childhood and you told me that your parents were never there. I asked you what impact you felt that had on you."

Elizabeth sat straight-faced. She did not trust this annoying, chirping pixie who was trying to unlock her dark thoughts.

Angelica waited patiently for a response, the silence between them weighty.

"There was no impact. End of story."

Elizabeth wanted to shut her down.

"Your son, William, is serving seventeen years. How does that make you feel?"

And there it was. A flash of hostile anger went across her face. An unguarded moment.

Angelica asked the next question gently. She wanted to see if this was the dismissive emotionally-unavailable mother that the press had created.

"What kind of mother were you to your son when he was growing up?"

Elizabeth knew the answer and remained silent. She'd had very little tolerance for the boy.

Chapter Twenty
Seventeen Years Later – 2021

I throw the newspaper down in disgust. I've just seen the obituaries. It is ironic that William's treasured mother finally passed away aged seventy-two years. It is a shame she hadn't died a week earlier when William was inside. Every fibre within me feels annoyed to think he probably shared her final hours. The woman who entrapped me. My life has been screwed up every day since. I hope she suffered. I hope William is inconsolable with grief but I doubt it. He doesn't have any empathy in him.

I have read about his release, online. Old news to most people. The piece said that 51-year-old William Channing was being released from prison, having served nearly seventeen years for the murders of 18-year-old Helen Boleyn and 27-year-old Rebecca Bixby, and the kidnap of 28-year-old Faith Taylor. I have read the news every day, for nearly seventeen years, for updates on the man I'm going to kill.

I can remember those days as if they had happened yesterday. Imprisoned by him and his mother for two weeks. It felt so much longer.

The police haven't informed me of his release. No one knows where or who I am. I am back living in England with Agatha, secure in our home. I stretch out on my couch and my thoughts turn to those days. Pebbles, my cat, curls up beside me. Her ears move slightly as I shift my position on the couch but she doesn't budge. I never told my parents that

William had butchered Snowy. It was best not to torment them any more.

I decorated this room. Everything is clean and fresh. The colour scheme for the living room is white with shades of grey. Sunlight floods in and it is a striking contrast to my time spent with a murderer. My days include hours of cleaning as I must have everything clean and in its place. The opposite of that room.

I remember waking up in the hospital; feeling the relief, feeling clean. I had deeply cut my left leg and arm on the window. Faint scars remain from the forty stitches. I'd stayed in the hospital for seven days with my parents visiting twice a day, every day. Then it was a tiresome week of interviews with the police. The media was relentless. The story appeared again in the nationals and I also appeared on a couple of talk shows after the trial. Financially I gained, mentally I was a mess.

I'd been in the hospital for about three days when the police spoke to me about Rebecca. She had to be identified by dental records. They told me that tests had shown she'd died before the fire started. They interviewed me for hours. I knew I was responsible for her body being burned beyond recognition in the fire. I said I was drugged and couldn't remember how the fire had started. William had given me an old electric heater as the room was so cold. It must have fallen.

After four months of being released from the hospital, I left the country and moved to France where I stayed for about a year until I had to come back for the trial. My parents had friends, Helena and Philip Carman, who owned a small vineyard. They had emigrated ten years previously, having made their money in property. They picked me up from the ferry terminal in Calais. I was to help them on their land.

A few days after settling in, I discovered something that altered my life forever. Months of isolation followed. I rarely left my room. I was too scared. I never worked the land and my parents sent money to the Carmans to cover my board and lodging.

Helena recommended thérapie. I went to three sessions then never went back. Nearly five months after my capture, I couldn't deny it anymore. I was pregnant with a predator's child.

The Carmans promised to keep my secret. As my stomach grew, I ran through my options. I'd left it too long for a termination, which left either to keep a reminder of William or put the baby up for adoption. As the weeks ticked by and my stomach grew, I didn't allow myself to think of the innocent life growing within me as my child. My son or daughter.

Three months later, and three weeks earlier than expected, I gave birth in my room. The Carmans had arranged for me to see a retired midwife, Madame Audry, about six months into my pregnancy. I was grateful for her gentle calm presence as she delivered 6lb 13oz Agatha Rebecca Taylor into the world. We lived in France for ten years.

I had returned briefly for three months for the trial while Agatha stayed with the Carmans. Back in the North East of England, my life became unbearable. Everybody and anybody wanted to know how I felt. I kept the birth a secret. I'd never been sure if he had raped me that first night. Now I had proof.

When I first left the hospital, I'd been interviewed under caution about the fire. I told the truth, in part. I described the room, the dampness, the cold, my fear and the isolation. I explained that William had given me a newspaper to read and an electric heater. The newspaper must have fallen onto the heater. The arson charge was dropped.

My parents had kept the newspapers which covered the story of my escape. I had read, with irritation, the piece on Aidan Handford being killed that same night in a car accident. There was a photo of him and his devastated fiancée, Imogen Fernsby. Fiancée! I liked him but he had wasted no time getting engaged.

Another example of irony. The paper mentioned that Imogen Fernsby had been covering the story of my disappearance. I wonder if she knew I'd been meeting Aidan for lunch.

A cold icy feeling crept over my body when I read that there was a family connection between Aidan and William. Aidan had an aunt, Dorothy Heist, who was the sister of Elizabeth Channing, William's mother. William was his second cousin. I feel my destiny may have taken me to William even if I had ignored his mother's plea for help.

After the trial and before heading back to the sanctuary of the Carmans' vineyard, everybody and anybody wanted to have their say. Telling me to forget it all, I'm strong, to move on with my life. My therapist supported me through the trial and talked about the importance of letting go of my anger and putting the kidnap behind me. I didn't find it that easy. But I have dealt with it, in my way. Planning for the day when William is released. No matter how many years go by, I am waiting and I am ready.

His mother, Elizabeth Channing, served three years of a six-year sentence for the manslaughter of her husband. It should have been longer and for murder. But, thanks to a risk-averse snowflake jury, it wasn't to be. Unbelievably, there were no charges for her part in my abduction. She sat in the dock giving a star performance of an elderly woman with a heart condition, which had been confirmed by an independent doctor. Her solicitor, Octavia Olympia, a small fat badly-dressed narcissist, had summed up to the court that her client hadn't known I was still in the house. I had unwittingly supported her plea of innocence when I confirmed she'd never brought me food and I could not be one hundred per cent certain that I had seen her in the room. Elizabeth Channing had testified that she had taken a bad turn in the street and had been helped by the alleged victim. She had taken her back to the house. Her doctor had testified that, yes, Mrs Channing had a heart condition. Yes, a symptom could be dizzy spells.

The jury bought it and there was no evidence to convict his mother of entrapment. William also testified that his mother knew nothing. He had covered for her and she served only half her sentence.

At the trial a police officer testified they had actually spoken to Elizabeth Channing as part of their house-to-house enquiries. The run down, housing estate was near to the metro station the victim had used to commute only three days earlier. Faith had actually lay upstairs drugged whilst Elizabeth gave a very convincing performance of a sane, sweet lady who hadn't seen anything or anyone.

William also confessed to the murder of Helen Boleyn, to save his mother from serving extra time. She had stabbed the 18-year-old budding actress just because she could. The police had found Helen's body buried on top of his father's. He was relieved that they haven't dug the rest of the garden up, with its thick brambles and six-foot-long weeds. They would have found a few more.

*

William's release has unleashed all the hurt and hatred that festers within me. As I approach forty-five years of age, I have never married. I want to remain anonymous and unseen. My blonde hair is now natural brown, mixed with the odd grey hair. My soporific life has changed my slim figure. It's now rounded, even plump. I can't help being blamed for the way my life has turned out and how I look at the abduction. Plain people have to work harder at life than attractive ones. I would describe myself as plain now. People leave me alone and no one gives me a second glance, even when I do go out on rare occasions.

Over the years, I have generated a revenge list of possible ways to end William's life. I have thought of poisoning, stabbing or running him over, but I want something that takes time. Something where he knows he will die and that I am responsible.

My parents tried to help me but I wouldn't listen, and I turned my back on them. They are, after all, my adoptive parents. They aren't my flesh and blood. I don't know the names of my birth parents and I don't care. Slowly, over the years I have become a recluse. Forgotten by the media and my old friends.

I still can't abide untidiness, old newspapers or dirty cups. It reminds me too much of William's house. My house is spotless; it is an obsession. My groceries are delivered along with a daily newspaper. Months pass and I rarely leave the house. My connection with the outside world is the Internet. Everything I need is online, including information.

I have waited. Patiently planning. Waiting for the day William will return. That day is here. I feel a strange excitement as the waiting is nearly over. I know what I must do. I've had seventeen years to plan it. I have the perfect venue, transport and motive. I definitely have a motive.

I'm ready to play. This time, I'm not the victim, which excites me.

Chapter Twenty-One

It's a beautiful day. Apart from sitting in my private garden at my farmhouse, I don't often get to feel the sun. I like to watch it fill my front room with light and brightness. My safe space. It is very warm for only 11 am on a September morning.

After nearly two decades, I'm so near yet so far from William. He's wearing his signature grey trench coat and trilby hat. This time I am watching him. Hunting him. He doesn't know I'm here. I feel powerful. Watching from deep within the cemetery, I shadow him. He and the priest are at his mother's graveside. I wonder if the young handsome priest knows how evil he is.

I can just make out the large pile of earth next to the open grave, covered with some sort of green material. Bending down, I place a carnation I stole earlier from another grave. I don't know who Mary Kelly was, but she died in 1953, aged 31, wife of Marlow. It doesn't matter, as I clean away the weeds. I am doing what I now do best. Blending in.

Raising myself slightly, I see the priest and William start to walk away from the graveside. Two men dressed in black trousers and green tops stand back discreetly, waiting to fill in the grave. After shaking hands with the man of God, William climbs into the back of the waiting hearse. I wait a moment before making my way to the private road, back to the waiting taxi and climb into the back seat. My car is parked about two miles away.

"Where to now, Love?"

I study the taxi driver's eyes in the rear-view mirror. Dull brown eyes. Tired eyes. He has no idea who I am or what I am about to become.

"Just drive, please. I will give you directions as we go. I'd like to see more of the area."

Street after street passes by. I watch the world from the safety of the back of the taxi. We pass a group of loud youths trying to jostle each other onto the road, laughing as they do so. I have become so judgmental over these empty years. They will probably all end up doing nothing with their lives. Waste of space, the lot of them.

I'm aware that years of negative thoughts have left me with pessimistic beliefs and feelings. I expect things to go wrong. I focus on the negative aspects of a situation, waiting for things to turn out for the worst. Yet, I describe myself as a realist. I will never be caught off-guard again. I have a backup plan for everything.

"Next left, please," I instruct the dull-eyed driver, "then straight on."

Up ahead, William leaves the funeral car. A lone figure, he heads towards a smart Victorian-looking house. As we drive past, I can see it's a B&B. Smiling contently, I give the taxi driver the name of a street a short walk from my car, content in the knowledge I know where William is staying.

He is about to experience what I have spent years planning.

*

Entering the grand house, William headed for his room. There were three floors and his room was situated on the first. In its day, the carpet would have had a deep rich red pile but it had thinned after years of heavy footfall. The walls, decorated in creamy ivory, would have added to its luxurious feel. Now the walls were bare, marked and faded. The heavy mahogany bannister was stylish but most of its residents weren't sober enough to notice.

Walking past three closed doors, William stopped at the fourth. Taking a key from his grey trench coat pocket, he released the lock. The room was large and airy and the high ceiling was decorated with an intricate cornice. So different to how he had lived before Faith ruined everything. The single bed with white bedding was one of only three things in the room. There was also a walnut wardrobe and chest of drawers. Both were empty as he wore all the clothes he owned. There was no ensuite. Just a shared bathroom. It always smelt of shit.

He felt drained. Images of his cherished mother filled his head as he lay on the bed, staring at the cornice. She was all that had kept him going as the years in prison passed slowly.

How he had loathed being locked up. He would get used to the way of life in one prison only to be moved to another and, with two years left of his sentence to serve, he was moved to HMP Frankland, Durham. They all had something in common, having a regimented routine and having to watch your back.

He had suffered during his time. There was a scar on his right arm where, six years into his sentence, an inmate had sliced it open with a roughly-cut lid from a tin of tuna. His crime? His personal hygiene. His cellmate had gotten fed up with the smell of reeking body odour. He never made friendships with the inmates or screws.

He would imagine squeezing slowly the life from anyone who spoke to him. Especially Daryl Sinnatt. A prison officer from William's early days in Belmarsh. Arrogant bastard.

Thinking of him made anger rise within. His brow creased with hatred. The humiliating strip searches, turning over his cell and always making him clean up other prisoners' shit. Literally. He hated him and was pleased when he had been transferred up north. For over a decade, their paths never crossed. Until William came across him on his third day of being banged up at HMP Frankland.

William knew he only had a few years left to serve and started to make it his business to pick up any information he could about Daryl Sinnatt. He knew he was married, had two grown-up sons, and had started his career as a police constable. At the age of twenty-five, he had transferred to Her Majesty's Prison Service. Now at forty-eight, with grey wavy hair and a small chubby build, he took backhanders and was no better than some of the inmates.

William also knew where he lived. He planned to visit him. It was payback time.

Removing his shirt and trousers, he dropped them onto the floor as he climbed into bed, not bothering again with a shower. He was thankful for the room. The halfway house or 'approved premises' was owned by a couple in their sixties, Mr and Mrs Forister. She had a professional air about her and was tall with short bobbed grey hair. He was tall, bald and charming. William took little notice as he had no interest in them.

Living there had been arranged by his parole officer and it helped when he went in front of the parole board. They were pleased that he didn't have any drug or alcohol addictions. He would be there for the next twelve weeks, then he had to find somewhere permanent.

Lying on the bed, he rubbed his eyes. His mind cast back to his beloved mother. He should have never been apart from her. It was all that girl's fault. In prison, he had spent hours imagining what he would do to her when he found her. How he would make her suffer and then end her life. The thought made him smile.

*

For the last few months of his long sentence, he had been let out of prison for eight hours a week, as day release. He had been based in the North East of England at a large DIY store. He had little interest in unloading deliveries or stacking shelves. He had spoken to his colleagues only when he needed to. They knew he was serving time for murder, and no one had gone out of their way to make him feel particularly welcome. He felt the work was beneath him. Too menial. He was far too intelligent to be wasting his time on DIY objects. Eventually, they placed him on the shop floor but he had no interest in helping customers. Every Friday he was there, he had hoped that his mother would come to see him but she had grown frail over the years and she never did.

His heart ached when he thought of her. The pain he felt was unbearable with constant nausea and pain in his stomach. He felt devastated. He was twenty-two when he first murdered a young girl. Trying hard to recall the memory, he remembered how he had watched her during the day but never approached her, and how excited he had felt when he heard her voice in his living room when she had helped his mother home, after one of her 'funny turns'. She had been his first victim, yet, as hard as he tried, he couldn't picture her face or remember her name.

How ironic, he thought, that Faith had been his seventeenth victim and he ended up sentenced to seventeen years. He had served fifteen for the kidnap of Faith Taylor and the murder of Helen Boleyn and Rebecca Bixby. Anger swelled within him as he thought of the lost time he could have spent with his mother, lost because of them. Lost because she had caused the fire which notified the fire brigade and the police. Something inside him told him that he'd find her. But first, there was Daryl Sinnatt.

*

William knew he had to be careful. The police were aware of him now and knew his style. There was also his probation officer, Scott Mathis. In his mid-thirties, Scott was a caring, everyone-is-equal, you-served-your-time and I'm-here-to-help kind of guy. William found him irritating. People weren't equal to him. He found that most people were stupid. A waste of space whose lives would amount to nothing. It had been a long time since he had taken someone's life. He missed it. He missed the control and power it gave him.

Daryl Sinnatt didn't know it, but he only had days left to live.

Chapter Twenty-Two

I've been procrastinating these last fifteen years. Sometimes we spend our lives procrastinating, thinking we'll start that diet and imagining we'll lose weight. Or we picture applying for a new job but never get around to it. Life stays the same. Just surviving and getting through each day.

Soon I will commit murder. It will be my first time. I'm excited and have planned it in detail.

Agatha Rebecca Taylor is now nearly seventeen years old. I still feel violated thinking that William raped me while I was drugged. Probably while his mother watched.

His daughter will be his downfall.

*

After the trial, I moved back to France and the safe haven of the Carmans' vineyard. Agatha was happy to see me again. Even in her young years, I could see she had some of her father's traits. To try and save her from the evil she may have inherited, I chose her name wisely. Agatha's name is of Greek origin and means good or honourable. She is neither.

By the age of three, she threw stones at Pierre, the Carmans' cat. She didn't like to be hugged and she told blatant lies. When I confronted her, she would shrug. There was no embarrassment of having been caught out.

At the age of six, her headteacher rang me to ask if I could go to the school. Agatha was sitting in the Head's office, happily humming to herself, swinging her little legs back and forth. Another child sat next to her. A beautiful child with raven hair and chocolate eyes. Eyes that you could clearly see. Agatha had cut the child's fringe, clean off, with scissors from the teacher's desk. Two angry parents were also present and her mother was in tears. I did my best not to laugh as the child, Adélaïde, did look comical. Agatha seemed to thoroughly enjoy the attention.

At that moment, I knew she would play an essential part in her father's murder.

*

She still doesn't know who her father is.

We relocated to England when Agatha was eleven years old and she is fluent in both English and French. An intelligent child who is very quick to learn and very manipulative. I can't wonder what her future will hold.

She is pretty but not beautiful. Blonde hair flows down her back and her green eyes are always watching, always analysing people and situations. At a young age, she learned to tell people what she thought they wanted to hear. She has a tall willowy frame; her father's frame. I didn't want her to have any resemblance to him or to have my darkness. Sadly, she has both.

Over the years, slow cold revenge on William has become my fixation.

I searched online for nearly two years for the perfect home which I found and bought at auction over the Internet. It is an abandoned three-bedroom farmhouse, with 1200 acres, in a rural picturesque part of England, in Northumberland. It had been vacant for five years and had just come onto the market. The roof had collapsed on part of the building and the brambles were growing wild and free around the outside of the property. It was perfect. I paid £300,000 in cash. It needed a total renovation but had electricity and water which just needed reconnecting. I had significant savings as the Carmans wouldn't take any rent, so I worked in their vineyard for free. I made and sold cakes and bread in their small shop and that income went into my account. I'd also been awarded a substantial amount of criminal injury compensation.

Sadly, while living in France, both my parents passed away. My father died from a heart attack when Agatha was only three years old. I comforted my bereaved mother by telephone but I didn't make the journey home for the funeral. I couldn't face returning to England. Not then. It was too early. There were too many memories of William and the trial.

My mother died two winters after my father. She had caught influenza which led to bronchitis. I still feel guilty that she was alone. I should have been there. I'd been selfish but I still wasn't ready to go home again. Their solicitor, Jane Edwards, handled the sale of their estate. My mother had left it all to me. Financially, I was very secure.

I knew that, when the time was right, I would return with Agatha. She would be living in the same country as her father. I thought long and hard about changing my name to keep my anonymity, but I decided against it. If my premeditated crime is ever discovered, I will accept the consequences. It will be worth it, as William would be dead.

We quietly moved back to England, one year after buying the farm. At that time, I hired a building company that supplied the decorators. While I was still living in France, they brought the farmhouse back to life. The transformation had cost £150,000 and every room had been painted white, as I had instructed.

*

Life moves on and no one pays any attention to us. It is a small farmhouse with land which used to be home to Romney sheep, known to local farmers as Kent sheep. Now the land is vacant and it is mine. I've been asked if I would like to rent some of it out for cattle. Maybe I will, but not yet.

The views are stunning, even in their neglected state. Just trees and grass. A stone wall, about six feet tall, runs around the farmhouse. It makes me feel secure. It's so quiet, we never see anyone. That's how I like to live. In time, I might buy a dog. Then I'll have a companion on my many walks. The nearest shop and school are about three miles away, although Agatha has been home-schooled.

She helps me reluctantly around the house and she's a great cook and baker. But she is at her happiest when helping to transform our land. She learnt her skills by helping in the vineyards in France and she likes the freedom of the outdoors. We bought a ruby-red lawn tractor which Agatha uses to cut the vast acres of grass.

We grow most of our own vegetables all year round and have ten white Leghorn chickens. Agatha sows and cares for the vegetables and I tend to the chickens. She has little tolerance for animals.

Next to our house is a stone outhouse. It must have been used to store animal feed. It's made of the same stone which runs around the outside of our home. It has a roof and concrete floor but no windows. I've had the door replaced. A solid metal door with a large bolt on the outside. At one time it must have been painted a brilliant white but now it is a dirty white with moss covering part of the walls. I haven't bothered to have the electricity reconnected. It remains in darkness. I love it.

It is the perfect place for William.

Chapter Twenty-Three

I preferred living in France. We have been in England for six years now and, at seventeen years old, I can still remember the vineyards, the rich smells and the feeling of contentment. My mum or 'Maman' as I call her, decided she wanted to move back. At first, I was angry, very angry with her. But, in time, I've grown to love the land. Our fields are no longer dry and brown, they are green and vibrant and they are ours.

I know very little of Maman's life before she had me. She never speaks of it. I only asked her once about my papa. I was eight years old but I still remember the coldness in her words and the anger that flashed in her eyes. Her reply was terse. He lived in England and, one day, we would go back so I could meet him. She could guarantee me that.

I'm still waiting.

Maman's parents, my grandparents, passed when we were in France. I had never met them. I thought they were already dead. When Maman told me they had passed, and their estate now belonged to her, I was shocked. Even more so when she said we were moving back to England. She had never mentioned her parents before, and neither had she mentioned my father or his parents. Maybe I'm going to meet them soon if they are alive. I'd like that, as there is only Maman and me. We are a very small family.

While I love the farm, I do at times feel lonely. I've always been home-schooled so never had the opportunity to make friends. But today, Maman said it is time I get a job and learn to interact with others. She has completed a job application on my behalf to work in a small café. I used to work in the Carmens' gift shop at the vineyard, so this is exciting. I used to serve tea, coffee and pastries too. My interview is tomorrow but I don't feel nervous, just curious about what will be expected of me. The café is nearly forty miles away but Maman said she has picked it specially and will take me each day. It will take about an hour to get there.

Apart from the long drive, I hope to get the job and, hopefully, Maman will tell me why she wants me to work there. Everything she does is planned to the last detail.

I know she is up to something.

Chapter Twenty-Four

Daryl Sinnatt admired his reflection as he straightened his regulation black tie. Not bad, he thought, for forty-eight. He felt proud of this thick wavy hair; he never noticed the grey. Turning to the left, then the right, he admired his broad shoulders and what he would describe as a portly build.

Striding from the hall mirror, Daryl entered the living room. His wife, Pamela, was proud of their three-bedroom detached house with front and back gardens and a driveway. Small, clean and cosy; she liked to keep it orderly. They couldn't have afforded it if they hadn't relocated to the North of England.

Daryl had told Pamela it was a work opportunity but the real reason was that he owed the local drug dealer £3000 and was starting to get death threats. He could afford to pay it as he had sold the drugs in prison for three times what he had paid for them, but he didn't see why he should repay Darren White. It wasn't as if he could go to the police.

Another reason was that Pamela hadn't been happy since their sons had left home. Nathan had gone travelling for three months to Asia, and Matthew was studying politics at Northumbria University. She was suffering from empty-nest syndrome and Daryl had wanted her off his back. Moving just over three hundred miles away and overseeing the decorating of the new house would keep her occupied. It had, and Daryl was enjoying his freedom once more. A bit too much.

Retrieving his house keys from the mantelpiece, Daryl headed for the front door. His shift didn't start for another couple of hours but Pamela didn't know that. He smiled as he thought of Sue Aldine. She had joined the team six months ago and they had been seeing each other for the last five. She was in her mid-fifties and recently divorced; game for anything. He had no intention of leaving Pamela as she looked after him so well. Anyway, a divorce would financially ruin him.

Unlocking the door, he climbed into his silver Ford Focus. The voice of Tom Jones belting out 'Sex bomb' filled the car as the CD player came to life. Checking his reflection once more in the mirror, he fastened his seat belt around his hefty belly. Pulling off the drive, he headed left and was only ten minutes away from Sue.

At a safe distance, William stood watching him. He remained still for a few more moments before beginning the forty-minute walk to Sue's house. He knew the way as he'd been watching her too. Adrenalin pumping at the excitement of what was about to happen, William strode on, with his head down.

Most of the jail knew that Daryl was knocking off Sue. With her sunny smile and dumpy body, she reminded William of a comedian whose name he couldn't remember. He ran through various scenarios in his dark mind of how she would die in the next few hours. He'd never committed a double killing before. It was exciting.

He was making up for the lost time.

Chapter Twenty-Five

Sue was waiting at the front door for Daryl. She greeted him, smiling and dressed only in a short red robe around her dumpy frame, smelling of Marc Jacobs perfume. She was excited. The sex wasn't particularly great but it was sex and it came without any strings.

Stretching out her hand, she pulled Daryl towards her for a passionate kiss. She could tell he was already aroused. Leading him up the beige and white staircase, she deliberately let the red robe fall from her pale dimpled body. She was about three stones overweight but she did not care because, at that moment in time, she was a goddess. Daryl loved her body and warm heart.

Entering the pale blue bedroom, they fell sideways onto the bed with their arms wrapped around each other. Daryl stretched his left arm to push the various pale blue cushions onto the floor. He hated extra cushions on the bed. Sue loved them; she had eight of them, all in various shades of light blue. With the cushions dealt with, he pulled off his clip-on tie and fleece and then fumbled with the buttons on his white shirt. Sue had already unbuttoned and pulled down his black trousers, revealing black and white cotton boxers which had been lovingly ironed by his wife. He still had his black socks on but they'd have to stay. He was now focused on Sue and her pleasure.

Only ten minutes later, they were wrapped around each other in a sweaty mess. Daryl was already starting to drift into a light snooze. He had just over an hour and a half before he had to leave for work. Sue lay, looking up at the ceiling. Unfulfilled, yet happy not to be in bed alone. She'd give it an hour before having a quick shower and heading to work. Although they would arrive separately, she and Daryl were on the same shift. That made her smile. They'd flirt with each other and sometimes he'd throw her a wink. They didn't care. The prisoners they looked after weren't getting out anytime soon.

There was someone at the door.

Sue's eyes suddenly opened as the sound of the bell interrupted her thoughts. She wasn't sure how long she had dozed for. Rolling out of bed, she reached for her red robe. Daryl rolled onto his side. He never got up until the last possible second.

That man loves to sleep.

Pulling her robe tightly around herself, she headed back down the beige staircase to open the door. She was expecting an Amazon delivery. It was a new black silk robe with a matching short nightie. She wanted to keep Daryl's interest.

Throwing open the front door, she stopped, confused. It wasn't the usual delivery guy, dressed in black and always smiling and carrying a brown box for her. It was a man dressed in a grey trilby and grey trench coat.

She froze. She couldn't move. Her body wasn't responding. She recognised the thin drawn face and those lifeless eyes. She'd seen photos in the media of him wearing those clothes and knew his nickname. She knew him as Prisoner Channing DH819733.

William Channing didn't hesitate. He was in her house and had twisted a rope around her neck, all in about three seconds.

Sue couldn't speak or move. She was at the mercy of the Grey Trench Coat Man and, for the first time, he was wearing black leather gloves.

William twisted the rope with all he had. He didn't want to kill her, not yet. He wanted her unconscious. That was how he worked and that was how he liked them. Sue's legs were kicking but she made little sound. Her robe had come open, exposing her large saggy breasts, tummy and pubic area. He stared at the large black triangle between her legs. All his previous victims had been slim and well-groomed. He'd never seen a naked unkempt woman like this before, apart from his mother.

She was now lying, exposed on the floor. He took the rope from her neck and tied her hands behind her back. He stood watching her for a short while. He liked to watch. Then he quietly started to head up the stairs.

He was excited about what he had in store for Daryl Sinnatt.

Chapter Twenty-Six

Daryl hadn't stirred. He was still lying on his side, with his back to the door. Gently snoozing, his body clock would wake him up in about fifteen minutes. Afternoon sex before the late shift had become a regular occurrence with Sue.

He did not know that the Grey Trench Coat Man was standing in the doorway, silently watching him. Enjoying every moment. For William, it was sometimes the best part. Watching his victims, feeling the anticipation and excitement fill his body.

Silently, he moved around to Daryl's side of the bed. Without a sound, he picked up the side lamp, while it was still plugged in, and raised it above Daryl's sleeping head. He paused to take in the moment.

SMASH.

With all his strength, he cracked the lamp on Daryl's head, then again and again. Blood flowed from a large wound. Daryl didn't open his eyes or respond. Feeling his neck, William was pleased that he was still alive but frustrated that he wasn't aware of what had just happened. Removing cable ties from his pocket, he pushed Daryl's body into the middle of the bed and blood covered his sleeves. Annoyance ripped through him. This was Father's coat. He didn't want to get blood on it. Anger was now controlling him. Roughly, he tied Daryl's arms to the headboard, pulling the cable ties as tightly as he could. Blood covered Daryl's face and was seeping across the pillows. No longer light blue; now deep red.

Storming downstairs, he roughly dragged Sue to her feet. Putting his arms around her body, he started to drag her up the stairs, with her feet hitting each step they moved over. She had started to stir. That pleased him.

The plan was not going how William had pictured. He had planned to terrorise them first by torturing Daryl while Sue watched. He had brought a knife with him which he had stolen from his B&B and had pictured cutting Daryl up slowly.

Now he needed another plan.

Dragging Sue onto the bed, he secured her left arm to the bed with another cable tie. It had to be her left as he knew she was right-handed.

"Wake up!"

William slapped her hard on her face and a large red mark started to form. She opened her eyes. She saw William and then Daryl. She screamed.

SLAP.

William's hand reconnected with her red check.

"Shut up, you stupid bitch."

William's rage increased. He didn't like loud noises.

"Please no. Let me go," Sue started to cry.

"He's not dead, if that is what you think," spat William.

Sue looked at the lifeless Daryl, with blood still forming on his head. He was as naked as she was.

"He's a bastard. He used to mock me and took bribes from inmates, thinking he was special. Well, he's not. He's about to die and you are going to kill him."

William's eyes were fixed on Sue. He felt no pleasure. He just wanted to leave so that he could clean Father's coat.

"Take this."

William put the knife into Sue's right hand, keeping his tightly around it.

"No, no, no. Please. I haven't done anything."

Sue began to cry again.

"Liar. You are both cheaters. You will die cheaters. Everyone will know what you are. Now, do it."

Sue shook her head, tears covering her face. William watched her for a second before taking her hand and the knife and stabbing it roughly into Daryl's large stomach. With a smile, he pulled it up roughly towards the ribcage. Blood gushed out. Sue tried to scream but William was quicker. He slashed the knife across her throat. Her blood joined Daryl's.

William left the room quickly. Not because of the bloody scene on the bed. He needed to use the bathroom as he had to clean his father's coat.

Then he would return.

Chapter Twenty-Seven

Agatha is having an interview.

I'm sitting outside the café. Big yellow letters spell out its name, Butterdish. It looks tired, just like the owner, a big middle-aged woman called Beryl. I've previously visited and sat in the window, watching. It is two streets away from William's B&B and an hour's drive from the farmhouse. He calls in every Friday morning and orders the same thing; a Full English with a mug of tea.

I've watched him from the safety of my car. I can feel the rage now. It never fades when I think of him. I want Agatha to work there. I want William to see her face; to like her and get used to her. She has no idea who or what he is.

It's all part of my plan.

*

It was so easy to find him. There was a small piece online, in one of the national newspapers, about his release, with an old photo. People had posted comments under the article. Some said he didn't deserve to be released. One said he looked like a guy living a few streets away from them. Another said he went into the local café and they'd seen him when they were out walking their dog. I looked up the area and watched and waited.

It was very early in the morning, on the fifth day. I was driving randomly around the area when I saw him, walking along the street. He was still wearing that awful coat and hat.

I parked up and followed him. It was a Friday, and he must have been hungry. That's when I first became aware of the Butterdish. William seemed to be a regular as he visited there again a week later.

The stalker was being stalked and he didn't even know.

*

She has been thirty minutes. My eyes watch the café and the street. I don't want William to see me. Would he even recognise me? I'm not sure. It's Thursday so we should be okay. I've parked up in my old Range Rover. It's a great vehicle for the acres of land I have but parked here, in this suburban street, it looks a little out of place.

The café door opens and Agatha is smiling as she heads my way. Her willowy figure is dressed in black jeans and a white blouse. They are the smartest clothes she owns. She doesn't need pretty dresses on a farm.

"She's so miserable. I don't really want to work there, although the cakes look good. She makes them herself."

Agatha is frowning as she pulls the passenger seat belt across her.

"When will she let you know if you've been successful?"

I ignore Agatha's remark about not wanting to work there. I am not going to give her the choice.

"She's got another person later today and there was someone this morning. There are only the three of us. She was impressed that I've worked in a vineyard and a shop. She's called Beryl and she said she's ring later today. Her husband has recently died so she needs some help."

Agatha sounds bored as she relays the information.

"If she offers you the job, take it. I'll let you keep all your wages and it can go towards driving lessons."

I know that Agatha will not refuse. She desperately wants to learn to drive. She wants more freedom.

"Okay," said Agatha, with a shrug of her slim shoulders. "I gave my surname as Hamilton, as you told me to do. What am I going to do if she asks for my national insurance number or references?"

"She'll offer you cash in hand. She looks the sort. We'll deal with that one if, and when, she asks. You need to get the job first."

"What's for lunch? Those cakes have made me hungry."

Agatha is now smiling.

I smile at my daughter. My only child. At times I have found it hard to love her as she reminds me of him. At others, like now, I love her; knowing that she is part of my carefully thought-out plan.

"Italian?"

There is a small, authentic Italian only a few miles from our farm. Turning up the radio, 'Killer Queen' fills the car. We sing along as we head off to catch Happy Hour.

Chapter Twenty-Eight

William stood for a moment, taking in the small, yet tidy, white bathroom. Scanning the unfamiliar surroundings, he found what he was looking for. A bath sponge. He lifted it to his nose and inhaled. The pink sponge smelt of shower gel. Taking it over to the sink, he held it under the tap and added some hand soap. Keeping his grey trench coat on, he started to rub vigorously at his sleeve. He could smell the blood as it spread into a large gory stain.

Furious, he stormed back into the bedroom. He had to expel his rage. Picking up the knife, he stuck it powerfully into the deceased Sue's stomach. Slowly, he crudely sliced her open from her stomach to the breastbone. Standing back, he took a moment and admired his handiwork. He could see her internal organs; the layer of dense white fat. They both had gaping cuts, with their intestines exposed. Daryl's bowels had emptied and the smell was overpowering William.

Turning away, and this time taking the knife with him, he headed for the kitchen. He was hungry and needed to use Sue's washing machine. He rarely washed his clothes. He knew how to but rarely bothered. He did not like washing his grey trench coat. He liked the thought of it being his father's so he never washed it. This time he had to, otherwise he'd be arrested again. Walking down the street with his sleeve covered in blood.

Putting the coat on a 40-degree wash for thirty minutes, he opened the fridge and started to make himself a ham and cheese sandwich. He was hungry and had time to spare. He hadn't eaten that day. The next day was Friday. He smiled. That meant a Full English and a mug of tea at the Butterdish. No one knew or bothered him there.

He didn't know that the Butterdish had hired a new member of staff. His daughter.

The washing machine bleeped loudly, letting him know the wash cycle was finished. Pulling open the door, he examined the sleeve. Relief. No sign of Daryl's blood. Carefully, he placed it into the machine next to the washer. He might as well tumble it for ten minutes.

While waiting for his trench coat, William headed back upstairs. It was the first time he had murdered a man, and with a knife. It excited him. He felt confident and turned on. Back in the gory bedroom, he took in the sight once more. The smell was still repulsive. He ignored it and headed to Daryl's side of the bed. He did loathe the man. It annoyed him to look at him, even now. The blood had clotted, forming a burgundy cushion across his gaping abdomen. Taking each leg in turn, he splayed them and carefully placed Daryl's free arm above his head.

Next, he turned his cold stare towards Sue. Taking her legs, he splayed each one to match Daryl's position. They were now a matching pair – completely exposed.

Taking the knife he was carrying, he placed it into Sue's hand. Bending her arm across her torso, he curled her fingers around the knife, before impaling it deep into Daryl's entrails.

He stood back, admiring the scene. He could picture the gossip going around the prison and he knew it wouldn't be long until his handiwork was discovered. William wished he could see Daryl's wife's face when his infidelity was discovered. Maybe she would want to carve him up too.

Before leaving the gruesome scene, he opened some of Sue's bedroom drawers. One contained T-shirts, another jumpers, and a smaller drawer was full of socks. All neatly folded. Moving around the room, he opened the dressing table. The top two drawers contained makeup. The drawer underneath contained what he was looking for. Her underwear. Carefully, he moved the lacy items which were in various colours of white, pink and black. He found an emerald-green pair and held them up for a closer inspection. He liked the silky feel and the black lace trim. He inhaled their scent, some brand of soap powder he was unfamiliar with, before carefully putting them inside his shirt.

Thinly smiling, he headed back downstairs to retrieve his trench coat from the tumble drier. It was slightly damp but not too crumpled. Putting it on, he pulled it around him, fastening the belt tightly around his thin frame.

Leaving the house, he left the front door slightly open, confident that no one would connect him to the slaughter. Most ex-cons disliked Daryl. It would take the police ages to investigate them all. He had worn gloves and was confident that he hadn't left any evidence behind. He had put his plate from the cheese and ham sandwich in the washing-up bowl and filled it with hot soapy water.

Another thing he was sure of. He had thoroughly enjoyed the last hour and wanted to do it again.

He needed to find more victims.

Chapter Twenty-Nine

Senior Prison Officer Ted Sabin was feeling on edge. Prison Officers Daryl Sinnatt and Sue Aldine hadn't turned up for their shifts. They were over three hours late. He knew they were an item and just hoped that they hadn't run off together. Picking up his desk phone for the fourth time, he rang their mobile numbers. No answer.

Looking up Daryl's personal information, he rang his landline. The phone was answered on the third ring.

"Hello."

It was a female voice.

"Hi, this is Ted Sabin. Is Daryl there please?"

"No, he's at work. Haven't you seen him?"

The female voice sounded slightly alarmed. Ted presumed he was speaking to Daryl's wife.

"No. He's probably on another wing. Sorry to bother you."

With a sinking feeling, Ted replaced the phone. His instinct told him that something was very wrong. He stared at the desk phone for a moment longer before picking it up again. He needed someone to go round to Sue Aldine's house. He needed the police.

*

Detective Constables Amelia Earle and Jeremy Sterling were four hours from finishing their day shift when the call came through from their Detective Sergeant, two prison officers Daryl Sinnatt and Sue Aldine hadn't turned up for work and no one had heard from or could contact them. Two PCs had found two bodies at one of the missing persons' home. Could they check it out? The next day was Friday and they both had the day off. The address was only twenty minutes away. DC Sterling let out a long sign. The paperwork would take ages.

"On our way," confirmed DC Sterling over the radio.

The drive was smooth with not too much traffic and the officers relaxed, chatting about what they were going to have to eat when they had finished and what films they had recently watched on Netflix.

Pulling up outside Sue's semi-detached house, they noted the small but well-tended garden. Two small conifers stood on either side of the front door in tall black pots. The front room blinds were open. Looking up, they could see that the upstairs bedroom curtains were shut, and the other upstairs windows were open. Glancing cautiously at each other, they headed towards the white front door which was slightly open.

DC Earle rang the bell before calling into the house, "Hello. Police. Sue, are you in here?"

Silence.

"You check downstairs, and I'll check upstairs."

DC Sterling didn't wait for a response as he made his way slowly up the stairs. There was a strange stench. Something wasn't right.

The first room he came to was the bathroom. Nothing looked out of place apart from a bath sponge on the side of the bathroom sink. It had a large brown mark on it which looked like blood. The stench was becoming stronger.

There were two bedrooms. One door was wide open and he could see a light blue duvet on a single bed and a white bedside set of drawers with a photo of two elderly people, arm in arm. He stopped in front of the closed door.

He heard the footsteps behind him but didn't turn around.

"Nothing out of the ordinary downstairs. It's all clean and tidy apart from some dishes in the kitchen sink."

DC Earle had joined him.

"It stinks up here though," she said, rubbing her nose.

Both officers knew something was terribly wrong. Wearing latex gloves, DC Sterling gripped and twisted the brass doorknob before gently pushing the door open.

Staying in the doorway so as not to disturb any evidence, they took in the macabre sight. Two naked bodies were splayed with the female's hand around a knife which was still impaled in the male victim's stomach. Both had been butchered with their intestines on show. Blood, urine and faeces spread out across the bed. The light blue duvet was no longer recognisable.

"I think we've found Sue," uttered DC Earle. "We'd better radio for forensic experts."

Chapter Thirty

It was finally Friday and Agatha was relieved. It was easier working at the Butterdish than on the farm. Beryl was okay when you got to know her, however, she was constantly miserable and moaned excessively about everything. She was paying Agatha £7 an hour, cash in hand until her trial period was over. Then she said they would review the situation. The arrangement suited Agatha as the cash was going towards driving lessons.

It was 7.30 am and Agatha had thirty minutes to butter fifty white bread buns before adding the sandwich fillings. Today, there was ham and cheese, tuna mayo and chicken salad. Beryl didn't cater for vegetarians. If need be, she took the ham out of the ham and cheese sandwiches. She believed we were all meant to eat meat. That is why we have teeth; to grind and chew meat. We don't need molars to chew lettuce, she'd say.

Once the sandwiches had their fillings, Agatha then wrapped each one in clingfilm, ready to be sold for £3.95 and, for an extra £1.50, you could get a mug of tea.

That week, Agatha had worked mainly on the counter, selling warm drinks, cakes and sandwiches. Beryl worked out in the back, in the little kitchen, where she baked amazing cakes and served up their best-seller, an all-day English breakfast.

8 am came and, at first, the café was quiet. Two elderly ladies came in and took the window table, ordering toasted

teacakes and two mugs of tea. Agatha took their order over to them, hearing their conversation for the first time.

"I don't sleep much. It's my knees. Keep me awake, they do," said the lady with a pixie cut. Her hair was ice-white.

"I don't sleep either. It's my back. I can hardly move some days. I've got a doctor's appointment tomorrow for my blood pressure. Sky-high it is. Sky-high."

She had longer hair than her friend. It was dyed dark brown but made her skin tone look harsh.

Agatha took a slow breath in.

What is it with elderly people and their long list of ailments?

She wanted to throw the hot tea at them and tell them to shut up and get out. She had had enough of Beryl's whingeing and whining. Instead, she gave them a thin smile, hoping to get a tip before they left. Beryl let her keep any tips she made. It was £30 an hour for a driving lesson and she wanted to learn to drive badly. Currently, her maman was bringing her and picking her up from work each day. It was an hour's commute, each way.

The café door opened and Agatha moved her glance, from the whingeing and whining elderly ladies, to the man who had just entered the café.

He was spindly and wore an old-fashioned coat and hat. A grey trench coat and trilby. Agatha continued to stare, her senses alert. He seemed familiar although she didn't think they had met before. Removing her gaze, she went back behind the counter, ready to take his order.

William approached the counter.

Father and daughter met for the first time yet neither was aware of their connection. William was unaware that this was the beginning of the end for him.

He felt unnerved. He never felt unnerved but, looking at the girl, she seemed familiar to him. For a moment he just stared. He liked watching.

"What can I get you?"

Agatha forced a smile.

William said nothing and just watched her. Her accent wasn't local and he couldn't place it. Agatha stared back, waiting for a response. They had the same green eyes.

"Full English and a mug of strong tea with milk, no sugar."

William rarely bothered with manners or pleasantries. He stared at the willowy girl with blonde hair and green eyes for a few more moments. Then, without saying another word, headed for his table in the corner. Agatha took the order through to the back and gave it to Beryl.

There was something familiar about the girl, yet William couldn't place her. He had other things on his mind. Things that excited him. He wanted a good meal inside him as he didn't know when he would be able to eat again.

Today, he was going watching. He was going to find another victim. Slipping his hand into his trouser pocket, he moved his thin fingers slowly over the item he had there. He liked the feeling of the silk between his fingers, the bumpy feeling of the lace. He liked Sue's underwear very much. He smiled as he remembered their naked bodies, defaced and lifeless. He felt that his mother would have been proud of him.

Chapter Thirty-One

I am waiting patiently for my daughter. I am sitting outside the little café, twenty minutes before her shift is due to end.

Finally, the café door opens and out steps a smiling Agatha, carrying a small white cardboard box.

"I've got cream fruit scones. They are so good."

Agatha climbs into the passenger seat and holds up the white box as if it is a delicate thing.

"Hello, to you too," I reply.

"Sorry, yes, hello. It's been a busy afternoon."

I start the car and turn the radio down low. I want to talk to my daughter.

"Any interesting customers?"

I try to sound non-plussed.

"There were quite a few."

Agatha is trying to picture as many of the day's customers as she can.

"There were two young girls this afternoon. They came in and ordered chocolate milkshakes, and then spent the next half an hour ignoring each other and just messaging on their phones. What's the point of that? Going to a café with someone and not even speaking."

It must be a rhetorical question as she doesn't give me time to respond before continuing.

"There was also this middle-aged couple. They were so excited as they were buying their first home together and just had their offer accepted. They showed me the house on their phone. It looked lovely. They also left me a £10 tip. They only had two mugs of tea and tuna sandwiches. Let's think, was there anyone else?"

Agatha stops talking as she pictures her customers. I can feel my heart beating faster. Has she met him today? Has she met the man who I have spent over a decade planning to kill?

"There was this weird tall guy. He ordered a mug of tea and a Full English breakfast. He stared at me the whole time I was taking his order as if he recognised me. He seemed familiar to me too but I found him a bit creepy."

I glance at my daughter, who has now moved her head to see my reaction. Time slowly ticks between us.

"What was he wearing?"

I have to be sure.

"He was dressed from the 1960s. Had a trilby hat and trench coat on, in grey. He was dressed oddly and behaved strangely. All his movements were slow and controlled."

Agatha shrugs her shoulders as if she doesn't understand some people.

I am quiet. They have finally come face to face. I have never told Agatha anything about her father, or how she was conceived. Will the truth change things between us? How will Agatha feel, knowing that she was conceived when her mother was held captive and drugged? I take a slow deep breath and remain silent for a moment as I know that the next words from my mouth will change everything. Then I speak.

"He's your father."

Chapter Thirty-Two

Sue's house was overflowing with forensic experts and extra police. The yellow tape had been put across the front door and DC Sterling and DC Earle were next door, asking the neighbours if they had heard or seen anything.

Ellen Haden was eighty-three years old and widowed for the past nine years. Her house joined the other side of Sue's smart semi-detached. A fat ginger and white cat lay stretched across Ellen's emerald-green armchair. DC Sterling and DC Earle were sitting on the three-seater opposite. The room was clean and homely. They waited until Ellen had settled into the cosy chair. She had opened the front door with a welcoming smile.

"How well do you know your neighbour, Sue Aldine?" asked DC Earle.

She waited for Ellen's response. DC Sterling had a faux leather-bound A4 notepad, ready to take notes. Ellen ran her thin fingers through her curly grey hair as she spoke.

"We always say hello when our paths crossed. In winter, Sue would knock to ask if I needed anything if she was going to the supermarket. Is she okay?"

DC Earle hesitated before answering.

"I'm afraid it is bad news. We've found a female body which we believe is Sue's. That is all I can say at the moment."

Ellen looked shocked. Her thin hand covered her mouth and her eyes were wide.

"Is there anyone we can call to sit with you?" asked DC Sterling.

Ellen slowly moved her head from side to side. No, she didn't want to worry her daughter or her grandson.

"When was the last time you saw Sue?"

The voice was gentle as DC Earle had a soft spot for the elderly. She would stay until they had gathered the relevant information and she felt sure Ellen would be okay.

Ellen was thinking. She remembered everything by which radio show she had been listening to or which television show she had been watching. She smiled as she remembered and was pleased that she could help the nice police officer.

"It was three days ago, about 4.10 pm. Tipping Point was on. I like that show. I get so many of the answers right. Sue was heading out to her car, probably heading off to work. I waved at her from my chair."

"What about today? Did you hear anything at all, or see anyone go into Sue's?"

It was DC Sterling who spoke at that time. He wanted to get away and call at a few more houses.

"No, Apollo and I had a nap this afternoon. We haven't seen anyone."

Ellen moved her head back slightly to smile at the still-sleeping ginger and white Apollo.

"Sometimes her boyfriend, Daryl, is there. Then I can hear them! To be young again," she chuckled.

"Do you know his surname?" asked DC Earle.

"No, sorry."

Ellen had a look of concentration on her thin, pale face. She shook her head to confirm that she didn't know. DC Sterling was just finishing off his notes as he spoke.

"We have to go now. Thank you for your time. If you do think of anything, just call us on this number," he said, handing Ellen a small leaflet with police information and his telephone number and extension.

"Thank you for your time. Are you okay?" enquired DC Earle.

"I'm okay. I'm going to have a sandwich and watch Coronation Street. Aren't we, Apollo? Apollo likes tuna."

Ellen slowly lifted herself from the chair to show her two guests to the door. She liked receiving visitors. She didn't get too many these days. Opening the door, she stood to the side to let the DCs step out.

They still had her backs towards her when she remembered something. After her nap, she had got out of her chair to use the bathroom. She had forgotten that fact earlier as she hadn't been watching television or listening to the radio.

"I saw a man going into Sue's earlier. I saw him from my bedroom window. I went in there after using the bathroom as I wanted to close the window. A tall man, he seemed very thin. A tall man wearing a grey trilby hat and grey trench coat. Does that help?"

Both DCs turned and walked back into Ellen's house.

Ellen felt happy. She would be able to answer any questions the DCs had. She had seen the Grey Trench Coat Man before that day. She had seen him a couple of times standing in the street, just watching. Watching Sue's house.

Chapter Thirty-Three

William returned to his accommodation. As expected, it was quiet with no other residents around. Although some were on a tag, they would have to be back before 7 pm.

Throwing his trench coat, gloves and trilby on the floor, he lay down on the bed to reflect on the previous day. He was confident that he hadn't left any prints behind at Sue Aldine's house but he knew that the police would eventually hunt him down. He'd watched a few documentaries in prison and was fascinated by how DNA worked. He hoped his trilby had stopped any hair from being left behind. He didn't want to go back to prison as he had found most of the other inmates weird. Not right in the head.

He reviewed his day. That girl from the Butterdish Café seemed familiar yet he couldn't place her.

William's thoughts turned from reality to fantasy as most of his day was spent in his head, fantasising and thinking dark thoughts. He pictured himself still living with his mother in their home where no one used to visit. If they did, they never left, apart from her. Faith. He could not picture her face or think of her name without anger rising quickly and consuming him deep inside. One day, he'd find her and kill her. She had kept him from Mother. She had him sent to prison. The bitch. He pushed the consuming anger away and thought about the new girl at the Butterdish.

If he was still living with Mother, she could have taken the girl home. He could have washed her face, fed her and watched her. The thought excited him. He needed somewhere else to live. Somewhere to take the girl.

Every second week, on a Thursday, he had to meet a parole officer, Nancy Grant. She was in her mid-thirties, a well-built brunette with a thin smile that confirmed she took no nonsense from anyone. She had made it crystal-clear to William that, if he didn't do what she said, he would end up back in court and possibly prison. What did she care? She went home at the end of each day. He was due at his next parole session with Nancy in six days. That then gave him two weeks to stay off her radar.

He wondered where the girl from the Butterdish lived. He had to find out. If she lived on her own, he could drug and keep her there. It was time to start watching her. He loved to watch his women.

Chapter Thirty-Four

"What did you just say!?"

It is said as more of a challenge than a question. Agatha's green eyes are wide as she stares at me. She feels confused as she had pictured her father as handsome, with a warm smile and fair hair, not creepy.

"No, he can't be! Why would you go out with someone like that?"

Agatha's voice is rising and shock is replacing anger.

I remain silent and indicate to turn left into a supermarket car park. Agatha's gaze remains fixed on my face. I pull into a parking space on the outskirts where it is quiet. Taking a deep breath, I turn off the engine. Neither of us speaks. An oppressive silence fills the car and the click of my seatbelt sounds like a gunshot.

I turn to face my only child.

"There is a reason I've never spoken about your father. That is because things will never be the same between us again."

I pause to look at my daughter's reaction. Agatha's face remains motionless, her eyes a fierce emerald.

"Do you want me to tell you about your father? It's no fairy tale. More a story of repulsion and disgust."

I wait for her reply. Instead, she remains silent and slowly nods her head.

I continue.

"Nearly twenty years ago, I was on my way home from work. It was a Friday and I remember that I was excited as I had a date with someone from work. Then my life changed forever. An elderly woman grabbed my arm as I headed to catch the metro home. She looked in pain and I can clearly remember thinking that she was having a heart attack or something. She asked me to help her home, to get her medication."

Agatha remains still. Not a word has left her lips. I continue; the memories are still fresh, still causing me suffering.

"I ignored my instincts. Something told me to walk away but I couldn't as she was old and needed help. I took her to her house which was in a very run-down part of town. She seemed grateful and offered me a cup of tea. I didn't want to seem rude, so I accepted it. I have regretted that decision ever since. My intuition was screaming at me to run, to get out of that house immediately. It was dark, damp and dirty. But I didn't. I've lived with the consequences every single day since."

I stop, as the next part of the story is the most difficult. I grip the steering wheel of my Land Rover. I want to feel grounded before reliving the moment when I came face to face with him. The Grey Trench Coat Man. My thoughts are pulled back from the captivity I suffered and into the present by my daughter's voice. The words are spoken softly.

"What happened, Maman?"

Agatha senses she is not going to like what is coming, yet she needs to hear it. Needs to know about her father.

"I ignored my instinct to run and accepted a cup of tea. It was poisoned. I had been lured to that filthy house for a

171

reason. About three months before then, a man had started to follow me. I'd see him on my way to work, during my lunch hour and near my home. He just stood in the street watching me. I thought he was watching me, but he wasn't. He was waiting for me. Waiting for the right moment to ensnare me. And he did. He had an accomplice. The elderly woman was his mother. As the poisoned tea took hold, I can still remember trying to stand up from the chair I'd been sitting on in their front room. My legs were weak and I couldn't. Then I heard it. The sound of the front door. I can remember his words as he entered the room. He said, 'You have done well, Mother.' Then I blacked out."

Tears swell in Agatha's eyes. She fears what her maman is going to say next.

"How long did they keep you for?"

Agatha sees the hurt on my face but she needs to know more.

"A couple of weeks. He would regularly drug me, wash my face, and stroke my hair while his mother stood in the room, watching. I think he must have raped me while she watched. That was how you were conceived, while I was drugged. He would only let me wear my underwear. He kept me cold and hungry. He even dressed as me one day. He came into the room wearing my dress and a blonde wig."

"That's really creepy," says Agatha.

"It got worse. He killed my cat and my best friend, Rebecca Bixby. That is where your middle name comes from."

I choose not to tell her that Rebecca's body was on the bed in my room when I started the fire.

"I eventually escaped by setting fire to the bedroom they held me in. The fire spread through the house but I managed to escape. Your father and his mother, your grandmother, were arrested. There was a lot of media attention so I fled to France before the trial. That was where you were born. I left you there when I came back for the court case. My parents never knew about you. I didn't want you to be labelled a rapist's child. You are my child."

Agatha leans across the car and embraces me.

"I am so sorry you went through that. It makes me so angry. I can't believe I'm part of him."

I hold my only child as tears fall from both of us.

"Wait!"

Agatha pushes me away.

"Did you know he would be at that café? Is that why you wanted me to work there? Is that why you said things wouldn't be the same between us again? You are going to use me to get to him?"

I nod slowly.

"I've lived with this for countless years and I can't move forward with my life, knowing he still lives. I've pictured and planned his death for many years. But I need your help. I need your help to kill your father."

It is a moment before Agatha responds.

"I'll gladly help you, Maman."

Chapter Thirty-Five

Detective Chief Inspector Aaron Webb was in charge of the murder inquiry of the two prison officers, forty-eight-year-old Daryl Sinnatt and fifty-five-year-old Sue Aldine. It was day three of the investigation and he was getting pressure from those above and the media for answers.

It was a gruesome murder and he had never seen anything like it in his twenty-eight years with the force. The last ten spent with the Criminal Investigation Unit. Social media called the victims Romeo and Juliet. Two lovers had been brutally murdered by someone jealous of their relationship. So far, DCI Webb had found no evidence of this theory.

He had interviewed Pauline Sinnatt, the wife of Daryl. She'd confirmed he didn't have any enemies as far she was aware and that Daryl loved her. He wasn't having an affair and she didn't know why he'd been murdered in Sue Aldine's home.

Some people thrive in denial.

The forensics department confirmed that the pair had had sex just before they were murdered. Sue Aldine appeared to be in no other relationship than the one she had with Daryl Sinnatt. It was widely known at their place of work that they were seeing each other. If it was a jealous partner, it would be Pauline Sinnatt but, somehow, DCI Webb didn't see the slightly nervous houseproud Pauline as a murderer. Her alibi was that she had been at home alone, watching Dickinson's Real Deal, while cleaning out kitchen cupboards. Her next-door neighbour, Emma Jolie, had confirmed seeing Pauline bringing the washing in on Thursday afternoon and her car had been parked on the drive.

DCI Webb believed that the frenzied attack had been psychotic. It was hatred and revenge, and his theory was that it was an ex-offender. What he hadn't worked out was, who had been the intended victim? Was it Daryl, Sue or both of them? He had two of his officers going through a list of those who had been released from HMP Frankland during the previous three months.

The statements his officers had collected at the prison, from some colleagues of the deceased, told a different story than Pauline Sinnatt's. Daryl and Sue had been having an affair for months. They had received a warning for getting too cosy in an empty office where they were caught on CCTV. At first, they had been put on different shifts but, due to severe staff shortages because of COVID-19, they ended up working together three months later. It was also open knowledge among the inmates.

DCI Webb was still waiting for further information from the forensics department, and DCs Earle and Sterling who were the first detectives on the scene. They were searching through video doorbell footage of Sue Aldine's street and those nearby. CCTV was being trawled through for any suspicious vehicles in the area at the time of the brutal killings.

He had read the report about how the bodies were found with Sue Aldine's hand around the knife that had gutted Daryl Sinnatt. Their naked bodies were left open and exposed.

Next, he picked up the statement of eighty-three-year-old Ellen Haden, Sue's next-door neighbour. She had confirmed she hadn't heard anything that afternoon and Sue's boyfriend was often at the house. However, she remembered someone else that day. She had seen a man, in a grey trench coat and hat, leave Sue's house.

DCI Webb stopped reading. That description stirred something deep within his memory. He had heard of the Grey Trench Coat Man before.

It was time to do some digging himself.

Chapter Thirty-Six

William woke early the next day. It was Tuesday and he was going to change his routine. He was going to have breakfast at the Butterdish Café. Usually, he only went there on a Friday but he couldn't wait that long. The girl with green eyes and blonde hair was in his thoughts. She'd been in his thoughts since the day he had seen her.

He had to have her.

Picking his grey trousers and a white shirt off the floor, he started to dress. He rarely washed or showered. He didn't see the need. Glancing at his wristwatch, he noticed that it was 8.30 am. She would be there, preparing sandwiches, cleaning the tables and taking orders. He knew because he had been watching her from across the road. He had watched her yesterday. He had stood in a doorway. No one paid attention to him and the girl never seemed to look out of the window. She just moved around the café, serving customers and cleaning tables.

Fastening the belt of his grey trench coat tightly around his waist, he bent to pick his grey trilby off the floor before placing it on his head. Covering his thin dirty hair. Next, he laced up his worn black shoes before heading for the door and the short walk to the café.

The day was cold and crisp. Not many people were about, apart from the odd dog walker who glanced, then glanced away. William had that effect on people. He made them feel ill at ease. Most people drove their children to school at this time and the noise of the traffic built in William's ears, as he headed down Sandalwood Street before turning right towards Charter Road. Not long to go now. There was a row of trees on Sandalwood Street and William watched as a grey squirrel ran across his path and straight up a tree with a mouth full of leaves. William tutted aloud as he hated animals. But then, he didn't like many people either.

There it was. The Butterdish Café. He stood for a moment. Watching. He liked to watch. The café was busier than on a Friday and half the tables were taken. She was there, the girl with emerald eyes. She had her blonde hair in a ponytail and wore black jeans, a green jumper and white trainers. William pictured her immobile, sleeping peacefully on his bed, with her arms and legs tied together. With him washing her face and brushing her hair. He felt the excitement within him build.

He watched for a few more moments before heading towards the door.

Chapter Thirty-Seven

Last night was a long one for me and my daughter. We stayed up long into the cold night, talking. I have told Agatha everything. I have shared the media coverage and shown her the brown newspaper clippings that my parents had kept. She read every one of them. Sometimes more than once, taking it all in.

Her father is a serial killer and was charged with the premeditated murder of two victims, Helen Boleyn and Rebecca Bixby. She stares long and hard at the photo of his mother, her grandmother. Thankfully she does not resemble her. She reads about the court case and the prison sentences. Elizabeth Channing was sentenced to six years for the murder of her husband, Albert Channing, and the kidnapping of Faith Taylor. William Channing was sentenced to seventeen years for kidnap and murder.

Agatha feels so much love and admiration for me. Her maman, her mom. Yet something else stirs within her.

How does my father feel about taking the lives of those women? Does it make him feel powerful? Does he feel any remorse?

She thinks about herself.

Does killing run in my blood? The thought of killing my father excites and alarms me. I has no hesitation in helping Maman, but what if we get caught? I am too young to go to prison.

I have explained the plan and the role Agatha will play. So many years to think, so many to plan. She now understands why we have returned to England and moved to such a remote part. A place where no one else can see or hear what goes on in our world. I need to show William that he may have preyed on me, but I am not a victim.

William Channing, the Grey Trench Coat Man, we are coming for you.

Chapter Thirty-Eight

William entered the Butterdish Café and sat at his usual table at the back.

Agatha had sensed him come in and caught sight of him from the corner of her eye. She forced herself not to look at him. Her heart started to race and she knew, at that moment, that the game had begun. The game where her father would die.

Forcing a false smile for the large ladies she was serving, she nodded as she took their order of two tuna sandwiches, two fresh cream scones and a pot of English Breakfast tea.

"Coming up ladies," she said.

Turning, she headed behind the counter to give their order to Beryl, who made most things by hand, while Agatha served and cleaned. Before returning to her customers, Agatha removed her mobile phone and quickly sent a message to her maman. She watched the two ticks next to her message turn green and knew it had been read. It was short and to the point. Maman would know what to do.

It read: 'He's here.'

Smiling, she headed over to her father's table.

William had been watching and fantasising about her since taking his seat at the white plastic table, which was set for two people. Now she was standing in front of him.

Giving him her best smile, Agatha spoke.

"What can I get you?"

"What's your name?"

William saw the smile waver as she hadn't been expecting him to ask that.

"Agatha. What's yours?"

"It's William."

"Nice to meet you, William."

She kept a tight hold of her order pad and pen. She didn't want to shake his hand. She didn't want to touch him. He repulsed her.

"What can I get you?"

William didn't answer. He just stared into her emerald-green eyes. Agatha held her nerve and tried not to show how uncomfortable this weird man made her feel.

"Would you like to go for a coffee sometime?"

It was another question she wasn't prepared for, so soon. Things were moving quicker than she expected. She stalled for time.

"Why?" she laughed. "I have coffee here and it's free for me."

"You remind me of someone but I can't remember who. I'd like to talk to you."

William's voice was low and controlled.

"How about you walk with me in about half an hour? I have a break then. I usually just walk over to the small park and back."

Her heart rate had increased considerably. She felt faint. This man was dangerous.

William smiled a slow and leering smile before replying, "That would be wonderful. In the meantime, I'll have a Full English breakfast with a pot of tea."

"Coming up."

She forced a smile before heading to Beryl with the order. Once behind the counter, she sent another message.

This time it read: 'It's on.'

Agatha looked at her watch. She had twenty minutes to make this work. She served another three customers before William's order was ready. She took it to his table after briefly stopping with it behind the counter. She served it with a smile.

"Enjoy, and I'm looking forward to our walk when you are finished."

She smiled again and then left.

William nodded in agreement. He couldn't believe that it had been so easy. A few more weeks like this, then he would have her.

The café was starting to empty as people were finishing their breakfasts. The next buzz would be at about 11 am. Agatha knew she would be gone then, never to return.

She checked her watch again. Fifteen minutes had passed since she had served William. She went to his table.

"I need to take my break now, if you want to join me. Just a quick ten-minute walk."

She waited for him to answer.

Rising slowly, he smiled and placed his trilby back on his head. He placed a £10 note on top of the bill that Agatha had placed on the table on a small white saucer. Glancing behind her, she couldn't see Beryl as she was still in the back, baking scones.

Heading quickly for the door, she felt William's presence close behind her. They were on the street.

"Shall we go this way?"

Agatha gestured with her arm towards the quiet street. William moved to her side as they started to walk, at first in silence. William was the first to speak.

"Where do you live?"

"Not too far away," she lied.

She also knew that her maman wouldn't be too far away. Rather than drive home, Faith usually parked a street away and waited for her daughter. Sometimes she would go for a walk, other times she'd go shopping. Agatha hoped that she had stayed nearby that morning. There wasn't much time left.

"Do you work, William?"

Agatha was watching him closely. He seemed fine. She felt afraid. Maybe this wasn't going to go to plan.

He didn't answer. Instead, he stopped suddenly. She watched as he tried to walk. He was staggering and seemed drunk.

"Are you okay?" asked Agatha, as she scanned the street desperately for a familiar sight.

William tried to speak but his words were slurred. He put his left arm out to steady himself against a small garden wall. Agatha didn't see the car pull up behind them but she heard it and knew who the driver was, even before they spoke.

"Hello, William. I've been waiting for you for a long, long time."

William's eyes began to close. He heard the female voice as he was pushed roughly into the back of a car. He was passing out. This wasn't meant to happen to him. He was the hunter. He heard her words just before darkness took him.

"I see you've met your daughter. You've done well, Agatha."

He recognised that voice. How could he forget it. Faith!

Agatha smiled proudly at her maman before they got into the front of the car.

*

"It worked just like you said. I put the Rohypnol in his tea but I panicked as it took nearly twenty minutes to take effect."

I smile at my daughter. Now William is my victim. I turn briefly to look at him, laid out on the back seat with cable ties around his feet and wrists. I watch him for a moment.

How does it feel to be watched, William?

I head towards the remote farmhouse with William's daughter, towards his death.

Chapter Thirtry-Nine

DCI Webb had just held a 7.30 am briefing regarding the murder of the two prisoner officers, Daryl Sinnatt and Sue Aldine. Forensics had found two stands of hair on Daryl's torso and in Sue's bathroom sink. They had come back as a match for fifty-one-year-old William Channing who had been recently released from HMP Frankland, where the deceased had both worked.

DCI Webb had done his homework after reading Ellen Haden's statement and was ready for his team's questions.

"What was his previous, Guv?"

The voice belonged to DC Sterling who, along with DC Earle, originally found the mutilated bodies.

"Kidnap, false imprisonment and murder. He got a life sentence and served nearly seventeen years. The media gave him the nickname Grey Trench Coat Man because he always wore the same grey outfit. He is currently on parole and, under the terms of the parole, is staying at 34 Bowes Avenue, CA12 4AC. Sterling and Earle, I'll send a team to pick him up, then can you interview him?"

"Yes, Guv," they said, in unison.

"Any questions?"

DCI Webb watched as the small team of officers shook their heads.

"I'll be in my office then."

Turning, he left the small meeting room to head back to his office for a coffee, and various meetings. Something didn't feel right. Years of experience had taught him that this wasn't going to be an easy case.

*

When William woke that morning, he had no idea that the police had found his DNA at Sue's house. With what now lay ahead of him, he would later wish that he was under the protection of the police and facing his remaining years in prison.

Chapter Forty

My heart is pounding, I'm not sure if it is from excitement or nerves. I have had over a decade to plan this moment. It is finally here. The farmhouse, our home, is just up ahead and I pull into the long driveway.

The sun is shining, the grass is a vibrant pea-green and wildflowers stand flamboyantly in their mass of colours. I truly have grown to love this place, originally purchased for only one reason: cold revenge. It is a beautiful day outside. Inside the car, there is a strong smell of urine. Glancing over my left shoulder I can see that William is still unconscious and he has pissed himself.

"Shit," I say to Agatha. "I'm never going to get that out of the seat. It stinks."

Agatha twitches her nose but remains silent as I drive past the main house and head towards the main field before I stop at the small stone outhouse. It is one of the reasons I bought this place. Firstly, the isolation and, secondly, this stone outhouse.

I take a moment to study it. To study William's cold bleak tomb. The solid metal door with the large bolt on the outside will not allow anything or anyone to escape. It is about two by three metres, enough for him to lie down. I turn off the car engine.

I turn to look back at Agatha.

"Are you okay?"

She nods.

"You need to help me get him out of the car. We'll take a leg each and pull him onto the grass."

"Do I have to touch him? He's peed himself."

Agatha looks back at her father but feels no emotion.

"Come on, he might wake up."

I say it as a command as I open the driver's door and leave the car. Agatha joins me as I open the passenger door. William does not stir.

I feel so much hate towards him, this man who entrapped and raped me. Without warning, I lean into the car, cut the hand ties and grab both his ankles. With the rage I feel, I haul him out of the car and his head hits the ground with a thud. He doesn't stir. Agatha jumps.

"Help me strip him."

Memories come flooding back of my time spent in the dirty damp bedroom of his house. When I woke from being drugged, I was wearing only my underwear. He had removed my clothes as his mother watched. I am now going to do the same to him. With his daughter watching.

Agatha remains silent as she bends down and starts to remove the grey trench coat after I free his hands. The famous grey trench coat which I will burn shortly, along with the rest of this psychopath's clothes.

The smell of body order invades my nostrils. I don't think this man showers. I discard the worn shoes, grey socks and grey trousers. Agatha removes the white shirt and I haul him onto his back. His bony lanky body is on show. I don't think he has ever had sun on his waxen skin. I leave the grey loose-fitting briefs on him. They are soaked in urine.

Walking only a few steps, I pull back the large bolt. I feel so good. This moment feels so good. The metal door opens slowly. It has an eerie feel to it and only blackness is behind the door. I can smell the coldness and bleakness of the space behind me.

"Take his right leg, Agatha. I'll take the other. It's time."

Again, she remains silent but nods and smiles at me. I can't help wondering if she is enjoying this.

My anger subsides and, for the first time, I notice that this skinny man is heavy to drag a few feet into the stone outhouse. His waxen skin picks up marks from the earth. Earth he will soon be buried under, but hopefully not for a few weeks yet. I want him to suffer. I want him to feel the fear of the unknown, and unbearable hunger. Both Agatha and I enter the blackened tomb, dragging him by his feet. His head is now inside the door.

"Maman, help me!"

I don't need to ask what is wrong. In the sunlight from the door, I can see the hand gripping her leg.

William has woken up.

Chapter Forty-One

The room was sparse, yet large enough to be furnished. A smell of body odour filled it. There was a single bed, unmade, with white bedding and an empty walnut wardrobe which DC Earle opened. It was empty, as was the chest of drawers. There was no ensuite.

DC Earle and DC Sterling took in the surroundings as their colleague, PC Edward Hodgson, entered the room.

Trying not to breathe too deeply, PC Hodgson updated his colleagues.

"The landlord said he went out this morning but he'll have to be back by 7 pm curfew. It stinks in here."

Neither of his colleagues responded to the last remark. It wasn't necessary.

"Did the landlord say where he thought he might have gone?"

DC Sterling waited expectedly for a response.

"No. He said he is a very quiet man, keeps himself to himself, goes out regularly during the day but is always back by 7 pm."

PC Hodgson checked his notes but there was nothing further to add. He wasn't even sure why he was reading his notes as he could remember every word of the conversation with the landlord, Mr Forister. Their shift ended at 7 pm so the night shift would have to bring him in.

"Where are his clothes, Jeremy?"

"I was thinking the same thing, Amelia. It looks like he has left ... apart from this."

DC Sterling picked up the only item in the room. A small square silver frame, no more than three inches across, which contained a photo of a white-haired woman with an unsmiling and stern face. All three gathered to look at it.

"I don't think he has left. I think that is the only thing he owns," said DC Earle with a touch of sadness in her voice.

Chapter Forty-Two

William woke with a raging thirst and a throbbing head. Then he realised that they were the least of his problems. He felt the cold ground beneath his back and heard the voices, female voices, her voice!

Panic surged through his cold thin body. He could see someone standing near him and grabbed their leg.

"Maman, help me!"

He felt the hard kick to his side, followed by another and another.

"Let her go, you bastard."

Faith would kick his head in if she had to.

He let go immediately, his hand going to his throbbing side. He felt confused, tired and scared. This wasn't right. He was the hunter and now he had become the hunted. He was now the victim and his mother wasn't here to tell him what to do.

"Come, let's go. Are you all right, Agatha?"

It was the female's voice again.

He felt he couldn't breathe and, at that moment, he knew he was a dead man. Faith was going to make him pay.

"Yes, Maman," came the reply.

He heard the clang as they closed the door behind them, leaving him in sleepy darkness. He tried to get up but his legs felt heavy. He had drugged enough young victims to know what was wrong with him. He just needed to sleep it off and then plan how to get out of this cold dark prison. He didn't want it to become his final resting place.

Sleep started to sweep through him. Something the girl had said bothered him. Maman. He felt his heart surge. He remembered it was French for mother. Faith had a daughter. The girl from the café. The one who looked familiar to him with her blonde hair and thin frame. His frame.

Is she my daughter?

Despite his frenzied thoughts, sleep took over.

Chapter Forty-Three

Back in the comfort of my farmhouse kitchen, I flip the switch on the kettle. I need a strong coffee.

I love this kitchen. Everything is white. The pans, kettle, work benches, cupboards and walls. The floor is slate grey. So clean and pure, unlike my thoughts and plan for William. They are dark and unnatural. I feel no shame or remorse.

"What shall we do next, Maman?"

It sounds more like a statement than a question.

I think for a moment before answering. I'm not sure why, as I already know what will happen. I have thought about this moment for nearly two decades. I feel calm and at peace for the first time since, as a young adult, I was tricked into that house. William's house.

The kettle clicks off. I enjoy making tea or coffee, as it reminds me of my happy days working for Mr Evans. One of the few nice men in this world.

I hand Agatha her black coffee in a plain white mug. Everything must match in my kitchen.

"We do nothing, Sweetheart. When he trapped me in that stinking damp house, he stripped me to my underwear and fed me very little. He would stand in the room and watch me, always after he'd drugged me. I could sense him there. We are going to leave him to rot and he'll die eventually from starvation. You don't have to see him ever again until we bury his corpse near the apple trees. No one will ever find him."

I stop talking to study Agatha's face. This is, after all, her father. A stranger to her but still her father.

"I want to speak to him privately before he dies."

I was not expecting her response.

"Agatha, no!"

I've raised my voice, which is something I rarely do with her.

"Yes!"

Her voice is also raised.

"You owe me that. You've kept his identity from me all these years. I'm the daughter of a twisted killer. A killer I have helped you to trap, just as his mother trapped you. Tell me, Maman, how long have I been a part of your warped plan?"

She's so angry with me. I hold back the words I want to say.

It was me who suffered having his bony hands wash my body, invade my life and rape me. I have no memory of that moment and I don't want to have. I push the thought away. I love my daughter, regardless of how she came into this world. I will do anything to protect and keep her happy.

I'm uncomfortable about allowing her near him on her own, but I can see by her eyes that this isn't something she is going to back down on. She'll find a way to see him even if I disallow it. That's Agatha; always searching for excitement, with a lack of remorse or guilt if she screws up. She is, at times, like William.

"Okay, we'll leave him without food or water for five days. His lack of body fat means he's unlikely to survive for weeks. You can see him then, briefly."

"How do you know he won't die before then?"

I hesitate, as I know the answer. I've done a vast amount of research on starvation. I know he could survive for months if he had water but he doesn't have any means to access it. He's lying on a concrete floor.

Within 24 hours, his glucose storage level will be in short supply and his body will try to replenish glucose by converting glycogen from his liver and muscles.

After 48 hours, both the glucose and glycogen will have diminished and his bony body will start to break down muscle to provide him with some energy. This will be temporary while his metabolism changes.

By day five, William will be losing weight daily, mainly due to dehydration and electrolyte imbalance. He has little body fat so his body will naturally revert to breaking down muscle tissue for energy, as it's the only remaining fuel source.

When Agatha gets her chance to see him alive for the final time, he will be suffering abdominal pains, dehydration, low blood pressure and faintness, along with many more side effects, including a heart attack or organ failure.

"Statistically, he'll be weak but should still be alive. I'm not negotiating on this, Agatha. You will wait for five days and no less. He's too dangerous. He's deceitful and manipulative and I don't trust him."

Agatha remains silent. She is holding her coffee cup tightly, staring intently at me.

"Promise me that you will not try and see him without me opening the door first."

"Okay, I promise. I won't be happy if he's already dead. Can I go to my room now?"

"Yes, you can. I'll make a big pan of spaghetti for tonight."

It is one of her favourites.

"Thank you."

Agatha smiles as she hugs me and leaves the kitchen, still carrying her coffee.

It's going to be a long five days.

Chapter Forty-Four

As William spent his first night, cold and hungry in Faith's stone outhouse, the police raided his bedroom at 11.50 pm to arrest him on suspicion of the murder of prison officers Daryl Sinnatt and Sue Aldine. The landlord, Mr Forister, let four officers into his building and William's room. But it was the same as earlier that afternoon. Empty.

It was the first time that William had broken his curfew and not returned on time, explained the landlord. Something must have happened to him.

Officers Grant Hamilton and Jim Reid exchanged a glance. *Surely, he's gone on the run?*

"Thanks for your help," smiled Officer Hamilton. "If he turns up, can you give me a ring immediately? Here's my card."

The landlord looked at the police logo and the telephone number 101 followed by extension 6643. He stuck the card into his navy dressing gown pocket, hoping he didn't have to call. Experience had taught him that he would be on hold for a while.

"Do you have a number for his parole officer?"

This time, it was Officer Reid who asked the question.

The landlord shook his head and replied, "Not offhand, I don't. Usually, they have more than one."

"It's okay. We have the general number," replied Officer Reid.

Making their way out of William's lonely room, they were joined by their two colleagues, Officers Stephen and Blane, who had been knocking the other ex-offenders up to check that William wasn't in their room or if they had heard anything. No one had. The usual 'I-didn't-see-anything' response.

*

As William lay alone, cold and aching on the stone floor, he was unaware that a warrant was out for his arrest. If he had, he would have wished that the police would find and arrest him. He didn't want to die. He had never liked the dark. Even as a child, his mother insisted that he slept with her. She told him many times that it was because he was afraid of the dark.

She told him that bad things happen at night.

Chapter Forty-Five

William woke from his dream.

He had been back at home and he and his mother were watching Faith, in her drugged sleep, lying on their spare bed; her body cold and hungry. His mother was reminding him that he needed to have a child. He needed someone to look after him and his needs when she was gone.

He had been smiling in his sleep. But when he sat up, darkness surrounded him, and his mother was only a distant memory. The thought that she was gone hit him hard, as it always did.

He had to get out of this stone tomb. The smallest chink of light came from the bottom of the heavy door. He moved towards it on all fours. It gave him some comfort. The darkness suffocated him and he wanted to see daylight and feel the sun on his pale skin. He was so cold.

He licked the ground at the bottom of the door, searching for some moisture. There was none. Only dirt. He wiped his tongue on the palm of his hand, trying to clean the earth and dust from it.

"Faith, let me out! Anyone there? Help."

Thumping the door with rage, he continued to shout. He stopped from tiredness and listened for a response.

Silence.

He sat with his back against the door. The chink of light at his feet felt soothing. The only noise was his breathing and the grumbling of his stomach. He couldn't remember the last time he had eaten.

If Faith was no victim, then neither was he. Crawling on his hands and knees, he started to feel around in the dark for anything that could help him dig his way out.

There was nothing.

Faith had made sure of it, months before he had been captured.

Chapter Forty-Six

I slept well last night.

One of those deep periods of sleep when you wake the next morning and you are still in the same position you fell asleep in. The other side of the bed is still smooth and untouched. It makes me feel good inside to know that William is suffering. To know he is trapped. I like karma; it feels wonderful.

I'm sitting in my kitchen. The sun is shining and the room looks bright and clean. My mind goes back to the days trapped with William. For two weeks, he had me in that room, so damp and cold. The bed smelled of urine. To this day, I can't stand the smell of mould, seeing dust on hard surfaces or having my environment unkempt. It reminds me of him. Each day I clean and, sometimes, I clean surfaces that are already clean.

Whilst planning for this day over the years, I would sometimes have gone into the stone outhouse and lie on the floor to feel what William's last remaining days would be like for him. The ground is cold. It bites into your back and hip bones, and the dust gets in your hair, skin and eyes. The blackness is suffocating. I deliberately haven't left anything in there that he can use as a toilet. I want him to experience the smell of dirt and urine, as I did. Part of me can't wait for him to die but another part hopes that it won't happen too quickly.

Agatha is very calm, seeing that I have trapped her father and he will slowly starve to death. In another four days, I have to keep my promise and let her speak to him. She refuses to tell me what she wants to say to him.

I wander over to the small television and press the standby button as I want to see the local news. The story is about our local hospital and how stretched the NHS is. There is footage of ambulances parked outside as there is no room for the patients to be admitted. I don't know how doctors and nurses work under such extreme pressure.

The next story is an appeal to the public. A photo of William flashes up. It looks like a police mugshot. I feel slightly faint as I hadn't expected anyone to miss him. I turn up the volume and photos of two prison officers appear on the screen. The police would like to speak to William in connection with their murders. A policeman is giving a statement and, across the screen, a telephone number to contact.

My head is whirling. I need to go back to the Butterdish Café to check if there is any CCTV. But first, I need to collect William's clothes and burn them. Then I need to clean the back of my car in case there are any fibres. I may have to break the promise I've made to my daughter that she can speak to her father in four days.

I may have to kill him before then.

Chapter Forty-Seven

DCI Webb looked at the evidence his small team of officers had pulled together. William Channing was a convicted kidnapper and murderer. They had to find him. Quickly.

They knew that William went out most mornings from the parole house, run by Mr and Mrs Forister, at 8 am seven days a week and returned no later than 6.45 pm. His curfew was at 7 pm. The Foristers confirmed that he hadn't caused them any trouble and his room was sparely furnished. When he'd arrived at their premises, he wasn't carrying a suitcase. The only clothes he had were the ones he wore, daily. DCI Webb shuddered as he knew that they had once belonged to the accused's deceased father.

About ten minutes from where William was staying, there were three shops; a hairdresser, a convenience store and a bakery. All had CCTV. Footage from the last three days showed William walking past at around 8.15 am each morning and then returning at 6.30 pm. Always on his own, always in the same grey trench coat and hat. It didn't seem to show anyone following him. There were various people in the footage; someone out jogging, someone pushing a pram and a dog walker. Nothing out of the ordinary and none of the people were on the footage consequently over the three days.

Forensics hadn't found anything unusual in William's room.

Further investigation confirmed that he didn't have, and had never owned, a passport so leaving the country was ruled out.

Where would an ex-convict, accused of double murder, hide out if he had very little money, no known friends or family, and no home?

DCI Webb was deep in thought when his landline rang. It was the call centre asking to put a call through.

"Hello, DCI Webb," said the voice. "I have a member of the public wishing to speak to you personally regarding the missing suspect William Channing. She has seen you on TV doing the appeal."

"What's her name?"

The DCI grabbed a pen and wrote the information down. "Put her through, thanks."

The words on the notepad read Beryl Monroe, owner of the Butterdish Café, and she was about to make DCI Webb's day.

Chapter Forty-Eight

Black smoke swirls into the day's clear sky.

I have thrown all of William's clothes into a metal drum, added petrol from the lawnmower, lit a match, and I'm standing back. If I could stuff his body in there too, I would.

It's 6 am and Agatha is still asleep. She naturally doesn't wake up until lunchtime. That gives me time to watch William's clothes burn and drive to the Butterdish Café to see if there are any CCTV cameras on the street we abducted him from. I push the knot of fear down as I don't know what to do if the police turn up here. How will I explain a half-naked double murderer, trapped in my stone outhouse? I do not want to be charged with attempted murder and sent to prison. I've lived a prison sentence in my head for these last seventeen years.

I head back to my farmhouse. I need a shower to wash the smell of petrol and smoke away. Before I do, I find myself heading toward William and his stone tomb.

Everything looks just the same. You would never know someone is slowly starting to die on the other side of the door.

I look around and there are only sheep, trees and green fields to be seen. I don't expect to see anyone. The sheep don't belong to me as I now rent the top field to generate a small income. I've also been asked if I'd be interested in renting some land to old Farmer Childs. He lives about five miles away and retired from farming three years ago but now misses his old life and would like to keep pigs.

I'm giving that some careful consideration. Pigs are omnivores and there are many stories of them eating dead bodies. One farmer, reportedly, had an epileptic fit and died in the pig enclosure. His body was found, partially eaten. I'm not sure how many pigs I'd need to make that happen.

"William, William can you hear me?"

This is one thing I haven't checked out. How well can someone hear through the solid door?

Silence.

There's no way he could have died already. He's only been in there just over twenty-four hours. I raise my voice.

"William! Can you smell burning? It's your clothes. Your image as the Grey Trench Coat Man is gone, destroyed. You're next, William. Soon you'll be gone too."

Still nothing.

I'm tempted to open the door. I want to see his reaction. I've obliterated his father's clothes, the clothes he stalked his prey in.

I also want to know more about two dead prison officers. They aren't his usual target. My hand hovers over the large bolt. I'll risk it and open the door.

*

Trapped on the other side, William was cold and ravenous. He stood in the shadows near the large door. He could hear Faith's voice and he prayed that his silence would make her open the door. His hands were slightly out in front of him, although he couldn't see them. If she opened the door, they were going to go around her neck. He too was no victim.

*

My hand hovers over the large bolt. I pause for a second. I had better not go in unarmed. I search for some kind of weapon, a large stone or a fallen tree branch but I can't see anything. I stare again at the door.

I want to speak to him, but my instincts are churning.

I hesitate again before deciding to leave it and head back to a warm shower and change of clothes. The last time I went against my intuition, I had helped William's mother home.

I have pledged to never do that again.

Chapter Forty-Nine

DC Earle and DC Sterling were sitting at a small table in a tired-looking café called the Butterdish, on the orders of their Detective Sergeant, Harriet Pickle. DS Pickle was aptly named, and DCI Webb much preferred to deal with the astute DC Earle instead.

It was late morning and only a handful of customers were in. Two young mums, with babies in prams, took up about a third of the floor space. Near them was a couple in their forties, smiling and laughing with each other. They were either in the early days of their relationship or were having an affair, DC Sterling had said, as they looked too happy to be married.

Beryl had joined them, along with a tray that contained two mugs, a teapot, a milk jug and two cheese scones with butter.

"I haven't got too long and, if anyone comes in, I'll have to get up and serve. I did say to your boss, for someone to call after 6 pm."

Beryl looked stressed.

"Thanks for the scones and tea," said DC Sterling. "We completely understand you are working. Once you said you had the information, we had to follow it up."

"Tell us in your own words again what you told DCI Webb. Sorry you have to repeat yourself, Beryl, but we need to take a statement from you."

DC Earle finished with a smile.

"Well, I didn't know his name, but he's been coming in here every Friday morning for about six weeks. He's a creature of habit. Always orders the same thing; a Full English breakfast and a pot of tea. He looked a bit odd. He wore the same clothes every time and paid in cash."

"Did he ever meet anyone here?" asked DC Sterling.

"No. Always on his own. He kept himself to himself and always sat at that table at the back."

Beryl was starting to enjoy herself as few people listened to what she had to say these days. She missed her husband. She had complained and grumbled at him but she missed having someone to rant at.

"When was the last time he was here?"

Again, DC Sterling asked the question and DC Earle took notes.

"It was Tuesday. He'd never been in on that day before. At first, I was confused and thought it was Friday."

"How did he seem?" asked DC Sterling.

"He seemed fine. He ordered the same as usual, and paid with cash."

"And that was the last time you saw him?"

This time it was DC Earle.

"Yes, and that was also the last time I saw Agatha."

"Agatha."

Both DCs said the name at the same time.

"Who is Agatha?"

DC Earle asked the question and DC Sterling watched for Beryl's reaction.

"Well, that's another mystery. She was my new helper, on a trial. She took his order but I don't think they knew each other. Her job was to take the orders and then bring them out to me in the back."

Beryl pointed in the direction of the small kitchen.

"I plated up a Full English breakfast and Agatha served him. A little while later, I had to come through when a customer shouted for service. She had disappeared and I haven't seen her since."

"Did you report it?" asked DC Sterling.

"Well, no. I hadn't taken a contact number for her, with her being on a trial period. She was the first person I have hired as my late husband used to look after the customers."

"Could she have left with him? William Channing?"

DC Earle's police senses were suddenly fired and she had other questions.

"Maybe, I don't know. I was in the back."

"Do you have any CCTV?"

"No, not in here, I have never needed it. I've never had any trouble in here."

"Can you give us a description of Agatha?"

"She's young, about eighteen, tall, thin, with blonde hair. She wore it in a ponytail."

"Full name?"

"Agatha Hamilton. I remember her name, same as an old teacher of mine."

"You've been very helpful, thank you," said DC Sterling. "We'll be in touch."

They rose from the table and headed for the door, leaving their tea and scones untouched. They paused briefly to let a dark-haired woman, wearing jeans and a navy coat, enter. Outside the café, DC Earle was the first to speak.

"We'd better do a search on Agatha Hamilton. Something here doesn't stack up."

Chapter Fifty

William paced back and forth with only darkness for company. He'd never felt so hungry. Even as a child, his mother would feed him once a day. His lips, mouth and tongue were so dry. Tiredness encased him, yet he couldn't stop pacing. He tried to create warmth in his body but his hips and back ached from the cold stone floor. He tried to think; to figure a way out.

Why is Faith doing this to me?

He thought back to the first time he had seen her.

He had abducted and killed sixteen other girls before her. His mother had killed one while he watched. It was what his mother wanted, for him to kill. How he missed her.

*

He could remember the day he first saw Faith. Tall, with long blonde hair and an air of confidence about her. He'd been taking the metro in the afternoon and late evening, for weeks, looking for someone suitable. No one had stood out, so that day he had woken earlier than usual and decided to try the early morning one. That was when he had seen her.

It was her long blonde hair that caught his eye. She was dressed smartly, with her head down, reading a book; the title of which he couldn't make out. He moved further down the carriage. It was busy and people were standing. Some gave him a look, longer than necessary. He was used to that with his unkempt appearance in his grey trench coat and hat. He would have blended in perfectly in the sixties or seventies but, thirty years later, he looked unusual.

Soon, he wished the weekends away as the girl with smart clothes and long blonde hair didn't travel then. Over the weeks he watched. It was week three when the metro was particularly busy and he stood so close to her that he could smell her. She was standing too and had her back to him. She wore a heavy-scented perfume. She was so close that he could have touched her. He knew it would come but that day wasn't it. He waited a few seconds and then followed her. She walked her usual way, heading into the city centre which was near her office block.

That day, she detoured and went into a Boots store. She seemed to be someone who knew her mind. There was no hesitation as she went straight to the aisles she needed, picking up shower gel and shampoo, although he couldn't see the brand. Then she went over to a makeup counter and chose lipstick. He waited until she had headed to the till before picking up the same lipstick which he paid cash for. It had been £15.

Outrageous money.

He rarely spent money as Mother hadn't allowed it. They lived on benefits. They never used credit cards. Mother had kept all the money from his victims' purses.

After his purchase, he hurried outside and walked toward Faith's place of work. She always wore black high heels. They looked so uncomfortable to William but she seemed to be able to walk in them as if she was wearing trainers. That day, he did his usual and stood opposite her office building, just waiting. When she stood up from her desk, he could see her from the street. He waited for a glimpse of her and then returned near lunchtime to follow her again.

He stayed well out of sight unless he wanted her to see him. He did the same in the evenings. He watched. He had enjoyed watching Faith live her life, visit friends and even go shopping.

*

She had been beautiful and confident but now she looked plain and average. The thought that she may have also suffered over the years brought him some comfort. He continued pacing in the dark and feeling the walls for the smallest drop of water. Anything to ease his thirst.

Then he remembered the day she had betrayed him.

*

He had been furious. She had gone for lunch with some guy she worked with. They had laughed and flirted together as William watched them, from a safe distance on the other side of the road. He had sat on a small wall and cars were neatly parked along the street. She wasn't allowed to do that. Have someone else. She belonged to him.

He didn't own a mobile phone and Mother wouldn't allow them to have a landline in the house. He'd had no choice but to leave her having lunch and walk home. It was only about ten minutes away. Mother would know what he should do.

Mother was in. She rarely went out. She had been sitting in her usual chair, surrounded by clutter that neither of them noticed. How he loved his mother and he would never accept that she just tolerated him. Controlled him. He had loved his victims too, or partners as he liked to think of them. He believed they had loved him back.

Breathless from his hurried walk home, William had explained to his mother that the blonde-haired girl, with whom he wanted to have a child, had betrayed him by having lunch with some man from her work. His anger had spilt out, along with his words.

Elizabeth had risen from her chair, kissed him on the mouth, and told him she would make it better. A couple of hours later, that same day, mother and son headed towards Faith's place of work. And waited.

William eventually saw her in the distance. After a brief conversation with his mother, he quickly headed back to their house and hid in the garden. That was the game they played. Elizabeth lured them into the house and then William would come through the front door. They loved to see the fear on the young women's faces. The same script, just different characters.

That's when my life changed.

The first night William and his mother had drugged Faith, he had carried her carefully up the stairs and laid her in her new bedroom. The bed was damp and cold, and the blanket was threadbare but Mother said it was good enough.

As she always did, Elizabeth had stood and watched as he undressed Faith. She smelt so good. He had put her clothes in his room as he always slept with his partners' clothes. If they fit, he liked to wear their clothes when he washed and cared for them. If they had makeup in their bags, he put that on too. So that he could be them, for that moment.

After he had fully undressed Faith, he climbed on the bed with her. His mother had stood in the corner of the small room, still watching. She told him that he needed to have a child to care for him when she was gone. She insisted that he had to do the deed. He preferred to be with his partners when his mother was asleep, and he'd sneak in and do it then. Then he could show them how much he loved them. He didn't want his mother to think he didn't love her. He only did it if he had drugged them first. Afterwards, he had dressed her in her underwear and left the room.

Mother insisted that Faith only had one meal a day as food was expensive. So, she went cold and hungry.

*

Faith had been their eighteenth victim but she saw herself as different from the rest. She was no victim.

He had now become hers and she would be showing him no mercy. She had left him to die of hunger, in only his underwear.

Now it was time for retribution.

Chapter Fifty-One

I leave Agatha in bed and head back to the Butterdish Café. I need to check if there is any CCTV in the street or if anyone has a video doorbell. I feel confident that no one saw us put William in the car, otherwise the police would have knocked on my door by now.

The story is also on social media. It seems that the police think William has gone underground because he is implicated in the murders of the two prison officers. That will buy me enough time to dispose of him. I've always wondered what it would be like to kill someone. Now, I'm going to find out.

I park in the next street from the Butterdish Café. I'm wearing my shoulder-length dark wig, jeans and a navy coat. I'm an expert now at blending in. After the trial, all those years ago, that's what I did. I blended in so that I wouldn't be recognised. Moving to France helped. I might move back again after William has gone and take Agatha with me.

I hurry down the street. It's nice. There are two rows of terraced houses with walled front gardens, and most of them look tended. There's no one around, so I turn right and head up towards the Butterdish.

I can't see any CCTV cameras. Most of this street has terraced houses too. It's a nice area so, thankfully, there's no need for security cameras. I slow my pace as I glance at people's doorbells but they are hard to see because of the front gardens and walls. The relief is short-lived.

I see a problem ahead.

A police car is parked three or four houses away from the Butterdish. I don't believe in coincidences so I head nearer for a closer look. My heart rate is rapidly increasing and it's not because I have quickened my pace.

The reflection on the large café window makes it difficult to see who is inside. I move my position, pretending to be interested in the window display. It's a display of various butter-dishes; hence the name. There must be at least twenty, with plastic bread and cakes on various stands.

I'm going in. I can't see any police.

Walking past the window display, I turn the door handle to go inside but I can't enter. A tall male and a youngish female are blocking the door. They are police officers. For a split second, I'm eye-to-eye with them. They step back. I offer a smile and head to the counter.

Somehow, I manage to control my breathing. A plump lady walks behind the counter, carrying a tray with tea and scones on it. They look untouched. She dumps the tray down, next to my elbow.

"Bloody waste. They didn't touch any of it."

This is going to be easier than I thought.

"Is everything okay? I saw the police leave."

She looks like she can't wait to tell the story. At times I love a gossip.

"Yes, it's fine. What can I get you? You can have a free scone, as I can't sell them again."

I glance at the scones. They look tempting but all I want is coffee and information. Maybe Beryl isn't the tell-tale I thought she was.

"Can I have a flat white, without sugar, please?"

"Yes. Any cakes or sandwiches?" asked Beryl, who hasn't introduced herself but I know her name because Agatha told me.

I need to keep her talking.

"You haven't been robbed? Is it safe to eat here?" I ask with a smile.

For a second, she just looks at me.

"Robbed? No, I haven't been robbed. I called them because I saw one of my customers on the local news. You're quite safe."

"Okay. I'll have some flapjack, please. Why were they on the news?"

I give Beryl my best smile.

"Police want to talk to him about the deaths of two prison officers. He used to come in here on a Friday."

I wait for Beryl to give up more information. She seems to be thinking so I remain silent.

"That's £4.75, please. I'll bring it over."

I go to my back pocket and hand over £5.

"Keep the change."

I press one more time.

"So, one of your customers may have killed two prison officers. Did he look the type?"

I know it's a silly question but I just want the conversation to flow.

"I get all sorts in here. The other week, a member of staff disappeared. She was my only member of staff. She was out here serving and just vanished. I've given the police her name and they are going to investigate that too."

"Can I have my coffee and flapjack to go, please?"

I need to urgently speak to Agatha.

Chapter Fifty-Two

Once back in the privacy of their vehicle, DC Sterling and DC Earle reflected.

"What do you think?" asked Jeremy.

"What about? The tea we didn't have time to drink? That scone looked nice," laughed Amelia.

Jeremy gave her one of those looks where words weren't necessary.

"Sorry, I'm joking with you," she continued. "I think William Channing is a nasty piece of work and had something personal to settle with the deceased officers. He has brutally killed them and done a runner. To where, I don't know."

"Me too," replied Jeremy. "Let's see what we can find on Agatha Hamilton. Hopefully, he hasn't killed her too."

"I think she has probably just walked out," said Amelia. "Maybe she didn't like the job. Her parents would have reported her missing otherwise by now. But we need to chase it up."

*

Back at the station, DCI Webb had called a lunchtime briefing. DC Earle had updated the small team on her and DC Sterling's visit to the Butterdish which the suspect had visited regularly on a Friday. He had kept himself to himself and always ordered the same thing, a Full English breakfast and a mug of tea. He wore the same grey trench coat and trilby hat.

DC Pickle had nothing further to add.

"A creature of habit," said PC Moore, who was the laziest and loudest of the team.

Everyone in the room ignored him.

"One thing the proprietor, Beryl Monroe, did say, Guv."

DC Earle paused a second to check her notes.

"A member of her staff disappeared the same day, around the same time as the accused had been in. She'd only been working there for a few days. Name, Agatha Hamilton, probably around twenty years old. She was getting paid cash in hand."

"Look into it," said DCI Webb. "I'm not aware of any missing persons in the last few days."

DC Earle nodded in response, and DCI Webb turned his gaze to PC Moore.

"PC Moore. Update please."

PC Moore shifted in his seat. He knew he hadn't put the hours in that he'd been paid for on this case. He'd been too busy with his online dating profile and messaging women.

"There's no CCTV of him at the local stations and he doesn't own a passport or have any debit or credit cards. There is no registered vehicle in his name. Still got to be in this country, Guv."

PC Moore knew it was a poor update as he hadn't reported anything new.

DCI Webb knew it too. He deliberately stared at the lazy officer and counted slowly to five in his head. The silence was deafening. The message was loud and clear.

"Okay. Thanks to DC Sterling and DC Earle, it seems that the last sighting was at the Butterdish Café on Sandview Terrace. The suspect doesn't seem to have any friends or family. PC Moore, it's time for you to get knocking on doors.

I want you to go and talk to the residents of Sandview Terrace and I want your report no later than 5 pm tomorrow. Any questions, anyone?"

There were none. The room slowly emptied. PC Moore was not amused as he now had to do some work.

DC Sterling and DC Earle also had a job to do. They had to find Agatha Hamilton.

Chapter Fifty-Three

I'm speeding on narrow winding roads and adrenaline surges through me. Prince's 'When Doves Cry' blasts from the radio. I love all eighties music. It was such a great decade.

I need to speak to Agatha and ascertain what exactly she has told Beryl. I didn't change our surname, Taylor, when I came back to England. I don't want to hide. For years I've fantasised about killing William and didn't care if I was caught and sent to prison. Now, that is the reality I don't want. I haven't killed him yet but I would be charged with kidnapping. I don't want that either.

The one-hour drive has taken me forty-five minutes. I lock the car and hurry into my farmhouse, kicking my boots off. I won't have shoes on in my house. Taking the stairs two at a time, I head for Agatha's room.

"Agatha, wake up."

I move to her window and pull back the white shutters. Daylight floods the room.

"Go away."

Her voice is stroppy.

I pull the white duvet from her head. Most rooms and furnishings in the house are white.

"Beryl, at the café, has reported you missing to the police. She said that one moment you were there and, the next, you'd vanished. What exactly, when you were there, did you tell her?"

Agatha is motionless. There is just a voice coming from under the cover which she has pulled back over her head.

"How do you know?"

"I've been to the café this morning. The police were there at the same time."

"What!"

Agatha is now upright in bed. Her hair is wild and crazy around her face.

"What if someone recognised you?"

"Why would they recognise me? It was nearly twenty years ago when I was in the media. The two officers today looked only a bit older than that themselves. Anyway, I don't look the same anymore. I look dowdy."

Agatha says nothing. She has seen pictures of me when I was young and attractive, and now I look tired and chubby. However, my spark has been relit these last few days. I've started to sing around the house and I'm not eating so much junk food.

"Agatha, answer me. What exactly did you tell Beryl?"

She pulls her knees up to her chest, still in bed, and thinks for a moment.

"I told her my name was Agatha Hamilton, as you told me to do, and that I had lived out of the country for most of my life in France, where I worked in a vineyard and country shop."

"Did you say which part of France?"

"No, she didn't ask."

"Did you tell her this address?"

"No, she didn't ask that either. I was the first member of staff she'd hired. She just wanted an extra pair of hands."

"Okay, good. We should be fine. I have another plan to get rid of William, if we need it."

"You've promised me, Maman, that I can speak to him before he dies. What's the other plan?"

"I've rung old Farmer Childs and said he can rent the old pigsty. He said my call was great timing as the guy that ran a farm about twenty miles from here died a week ago from a heart attack. His widow has offered Childs a sounder of pigs at a reasonable price. There are fifteen of them needing a new home."

"Pigs? Won't they be noisy and smell?"

Agatha doesn't look amused.

"Noisy? Yes. Smell? A little. But they also eat meat. Any dead meat and bones."

"You're so clever, Maman. What a great idea. You are going to feed William to the pigs?"

"Maybe. He's coming tomorrow to check the pigpen and discuss the rent. We need to keep William quiet. I'm going to give him the smallest amount of water, special water to make him sleep."

We laugh as we embrace each other.

Chapter Fifty-Four

Three days had passed since DCI Webb's briefing, and the investigation had stalled. There were no new leads and PC Moore's door-knocking exercise was unsuccessful from the investigation's point of view but successful from a personal one.

Katherine Parkhurst was in her mid-forties, attractive, widowed and looking for a man. Any man. Her terraced house was clean, tidy and furnished with antique furniture. Bespoke oil paintings furnished the walls. She had inherited a lot of money, thanks to her late husband's business. Shipping and selling cocaine to wealthy people. She was still learning the ropes but having a policeman on her payroll would be a huge bonus.

Manipulating PC Moore would be easy. He had sat in her house, asking questions about someone she had never seen or heard of. She couldn't help him. Yet he had managed to drag their conversation out for twenty minutes. She had watched him preening himself, brushing down his jacket, pushing back his hair, smiling at her and then he had asked her if she would like to go for coffee.

He's so unprofessional and overweight, with average looks.

But she put the biggest smile on her face, showing off her perfectly whitened teeth.

"That would be great," she said.

*

The media coverage has died down. Every morning, I switch on the local news for any updates although I know they won't report that they had found him. My fear is a picture flashing up of my daughter with the strapline, 'Have you seen this girl?' But it hasn't happened. Neither have the police shown up at my house. I begin to relax a little, apart from today.

Today I am stressed and I don't like the feeling. Today is day five of William's capture. The day I promised Agatha that she could speak to him, privately. I will keep my promise.

I have not spoken or heard anything from William in two days when I briefly opened the door and threw in a small bottle that contained one inch of water and Rohypnol.

*

"You gave me water, William. Now we are even."

I said this to him as I threw the bottle in his direction, the smell of ammonia hitting my nose. He was asleep at the side of the wall near the back, to avoid the draught that blew under the door. I was confident he would drink it as his survival instincts would kick in.

Later that day, old Farmer Childs turned up to check out the pigpen. He said it was perfect. The pigs will arrive in a week.

Perfect. Just in time.

Chapter Fifty-Five

Agatha is up early today. She has found me in the kitchen, having my morning flat white coffee and watching the news. Usually, if she appears at 8 am I have questions, but I know why she's here.

"You promised that today would be the day, Maman."

Straight to the point, no 'Good morning, it's a nice day'.

This is a big moment. William has been in there for five days without food or water. I know he's not going to look great and it's going to smell of his body waste. Not the best of circumstances for a father and daughter to have their final conversation.

"Come on then. If you are sure," I reply. "Bring that with you, please."

I point to the large black object I had placed earlier on the kitchen table. It's a powerful flashlight.

Agatha looks ecstatic and nods numerous times. I walk over to the kitchen dresser and remove the loaded shotgun I placed there a week ago. I found it years ago when I moved in. Various pieces of furniture had been left, rotting away with time. The gun and ammunition were in the bottom of a chest of drawers, along with old birthday cards and family photos. I cleaned it up and kept it for security. I hope it fires. I've never tested it. But it looks the part.

We are nearly at the outhouse before I speak.

"You must keep in the doorway. Do not go inside, under any circumstances. He's dangerous. You can have five minutes with him. I'll stand back so I can see you but not close enough to hear you. Do you agree?"

"Yes. Thank you, Maman."

We are at the stone outhouse door. I unlock it and draw back the large bolt. My heart is beating fast. I hope we don't end up dead. I feel that this is a bad idea, but there's no going back now. She would never forgive me.

I open the door and shine the powerful flashlight. Even with the door open, it's still dark.

What have I done?

William is lying on the ground in a foetal position. His thin body, is now skin and bone. He looks like a skeleton with stretched skin. His underwear is stained, his face gaunt and dirty, and his hip bones and spine are prominent. He must have lost at least seven pounds from his already-thin frame. The smell is stomach-churning.

He raises his head to look at us but doesn't move. I move the light from his eyes as he's trying to shield them with his bony hand.

Am I not better than this?

I could end his suffering now and get him medical attention.

What have I done?

"Hello, Father."

It's Agatha's voice. She seems not to notice or care about the sight before her.

"I want to talk to you. Is that okay?"

William pushes himself up to sit. I can see his lips are severely cracked. His legs are so thin that you can see up the legs of his underwear. I revert my gaze.

I hand the flashlight to Agatha. I slowly stand back a few feet, as promised, so she can talk to him privately.

She's standing tall with her shoulders back, wearing jeans, a white sweatshirt and white trainers. She looks powerful. Maybe she is dealing with this situation better than I am. The sight of William makes me feel shame. I have caused this.

Agatha is talking to her father. I can hear her voice but cannot make out the words.

I want to let William go.

Chapter Fifty-Six

"You look and smell like shit."

Agatha was straight to the point.

William stayed seated on the cold ground, with his scrawny arms at his sides, trying to steady himself. He looked pitiful. A stranger finding him would have presumed he'd been locked away for much longer than five days. It was his sixth day without food and only an inch of water.

He was in pain. Agatha could see it on his face. Without fluid intake, his kidneys were losing much of their function and, eventually, they would collapse. Starvation interferes with the gastrointestinal system, causing bloating, stomach pain and vomiting.

Agatha moved the flashlight slowly across the floor. There were three pools of vomit.

"You not feeling good, Father?"

William didn't respond. He remained as still as stone. The only movement was his eyes, blinking.

His daughter continued, "I used to wonder what you looked like. What you would be like, as a person. Maman rarely spoke of you."

She paused and positioned the flashlight near the ground where William sat. She too had moved it from the dying man's eyes.

She continued, "I used to picture you as a farmer, growing the best grapes to make some of the finest wines. I just presumed you'd be French. As a child, you lived in my head as someone tall and strong who, when we finally met, would give me a big hug and say you've missed me. Then introduce me to your family. In my daydreams, I had two sisters and one big brother. Eventually, we'd all be one big happy family."

The words, when they came, were quiet and mumbled. His eyes were closed. Agatha watched as he struggled to slowly lick his dried lips. He had tilted his head back slightly so that he could see her. There were about twelve feet between them.

Agatha defiantly stood her ground.

"What did you say?" she asked, turning her head slightly to listen.

William sat for a moment, in silence. He had tried to ask his daughter if she wanted a hug now. Trying to talk was exhausting. His body hurt, he felt confused and his heart was beating fast. He opened his eyes, trying to summon some energy. He remembered he was trapped, but the door was open. There was light and he needed to get to it.

Was he hallucinating? He must be. He could see Faith, She was within touching distance. She had bent down to pick something up and was leaving. He could hear raised voices.

"No, don't. What are you doing? Why?"

Agatha's tone conveyed her annoyance.

Why is Maman doing this?

Faith had entered the stone outhouse and picked up the empty plastic bottle she had thrown at William only two days ago. At the time, she had only filled it with one inch of water and Rohypnol. This time, she showed compassion and had half-filled it from the water butt, next to the outhouse.

As she went to hand it to William, Agatha angrily grabbed her arm.

*

"This is wrong, Agatha. I was wrong. I can't let him die like this."

Her grip is strong, but I've pulled my arm free. I step back into the darkness. The man I've hated, and spent years plotting retribution against, is sitting upright, watching me. I bend down slightly and put the bottle in his hand.

He tips the water up to his face. Most of it misses his mouth and falls on his bare chest. He seems confused about how to drink or maybe is too weak. I think he has drunk some of it.

Agatha is next to me and no longer in the safety of the doorway. I can't help thinking that William could be playing us both, and at any moment will stand up and overthrow us. The shotgun is outside, lying disregarded on the grass near the doorway.

"Get out, Maman. He deserves to rot."

Agatha grabs my arm again and tries to push me towards the door. Instead, I slip in what feels like vomit and crash to the floor, landing on my elbow. A pain shoots up my arm.

William takes his chance.

Pushing himself forward, he is on top of me. I'm pinned to the stone floor and his hands are feeling my body. He stinks. Despite his bony body, I can't push him off and my arms are trapped under him.

"Get off her!" shouts Agatha.

William falls quickly off me with a thud, but I can't see as it has gone dark. There's a hand grabbing my arm and I'm being pulled along towards the open door. I'm only a few feet away and I stop moving. The hand has let go. It was Agatha's.

She returns into the darkness to search for the flashlight, which she must have dropped when she hit William over the head. I can make out her silhouette. She is on all fours.

There is light. Agatha has the flashlight. She's angry.

"You will die here, alone, in the dark. It's what you deserve."

She yells the words at her father.

Once more, William slowly moves into a sitting position, with his ashen arm trying to reach his injured head. It doesn't seem to be strong enough and he is too weak to stand.

Enraged, Agatha shines the flashlight near him. I can see his face and my daughter's outline. I push myself up from the cold ground. I need to end this and I want Agatha out of here.

I'm going to get William some food and water. I'll keep him in here until I decide what to do with him. I'll get him a torch, a mattress and a blanket.

I have decided to let him live.

But his words, quiet and slow, change everything. My guilt vanishes. I stop in the doorway, watching the scene between them.

He is staring at his daughter and she is moving nearer to me. William continues to speak, his voice hoarse. But we can hear him.

"That day at the café…"

He struggles to say the words through cracked lips. He knows they are probably his last words but he is going to get them out.

"… you were going to be my next victim. I was coming for you."

235

Chapter Fifty-Seven

My stomach lurches and I finally understand the saying, 'My blood ran cold'.

I feel ice running through my veins, an actual physical reaction to the thought that he had planned to take Agatha.

Agatha is motionless.

"I felt powerful in my grey trench coat."

We remain silent.

William's breathing is slow. We wait for his last words.

"There was a small hole in the left pocket. It's where I hid my list, in the lining. It had all their names on it. Seventeen of them. Even the police didn't find it when they held me in custody. Now you've burned it. Thank you, Faith."

William sneers at me.

I jerk Agatha outside and slam the door. I can't bolt it quickly enough. I vow not to open it until the smell of death seeps under the door.

Agatha is still holding the flashlight, her face pallid.

"I told you he deserved to die. He's sick, but you wouldn't listen. He was going to kill me and it would have been your fault. You made me meet him. You brought him here, into our lives."

I try to hug her but she pushes me away and runs towards the safety of our farmhouse. I let her go and pick up the shotgun from where I left it only five minutes ago. It seems like hours.

My trousers have a huge stain on the side. William's vomit.

I look around. There are only sheep to be seen and Agatha still running in the distance. I unbutton my trousers and peel them off my legs, along with my jumper. I have to force away the memory of his hands on me, only moments before.

Walking back, in only my white underwear and socks, I head for home and a shower. I will drop my clothes into the large metal drum I burned William's in. I don't want anything he has touched. I'll burn them later today. It's a shame he won't fit in there as, at this moment, I would happily burn him alive.

Back at the farmhouse, there is no sign of Agatha as I head up the stairs. Her bedroom door is shut. I'll leave her for now. I need to feel hot water and shower gel on my skin, washing him away.

My bedroom, like the rest of my home, is white. I don't have an ensuite. The bathroom is next door with a large walk-in shower. I lock the door and switch it on. The hot water cleanses my skin.

How did I get it so wrong? What possessed me to think I should save William? I could save his life, yet even so near to death, he won't change. I can see that now.

What worries me is that Agatha seems to have no conscience about ending his life. No empathy for the shell he has become. As I shampoo my hair, I wonder if I have given birth to a monster. My dad used to say, 'The apple never falls far from the tree', meaning that a child grows up to be like their parents, not just in looks but in behaviour.

I finish washing my body and then switch the shower off. The white towel is soft and clean against my wet skin. It is time to speak to Agatha about how she is feeling.

To find out how many, if any, of her father's traits she has.

Chapter Fifty-Eight

William couldn't calculate how many days he'd been dying. He knew death wasn't too far away. He was ready to welcome it and even his skin had cracked open. He didn't notice the intense thirst anymore. He was too frail.

During the first few days spent with only darkness for company, he had pictured his mother. How he missed her and he hoped she was waiting for him, even though she didn't believe there was a God. He had spent his life trying to please her yet, sadly, he knew he had failed. What would she have thought of his daughter, Agatha; her only grandchild? Would she have liked her?

If things had been different, they could have all lived happily as a family. The thought that he wouldn't be part of her life distressed him. He couldn't comprehend that how Agatha had been conceived was wrong. He gave no thought to the seventeen girls he and his mother had murdered. All those lives stolen, all those families left grieving and speculating about what had happened. Their bodies were yet to be discovered. The police were only aware of 27-year-old Rebecca Bixby who William had taken only days after Faith.

His cold and callous mother had raised him to snatch lives away, without remorse or guilt. The excitement of controlling another person drove him to commit again and again. He was not sorry for the life he had led. He was only sorry for having to serve so much time incarcerated for the murder of a girl whose name he could no longer remember and for not killing Faith.

He could no longer open his sunken eyes. They were too dry. It didn't matter that his dusty stone tomb was completely dark. His body was shutting down. Fluid seeped from him, even though liquid had barely touched his lips in eleven days. His organs were breaking down. Body fluid and dust encrusted his underwear. The only item that remained from his old life. The one item of clothing Faith had left him with. Retribution for when he had left her for two weeks in only her underwear.

As his lungs slowly ceased to work, they released a thick substance that formed in the back of his throat which gradually choked him. He tried to take a weak breath through cracked, painful lips. His gums were swollen and his chest barely rose. Mercifully, he had drifted in and out of sleep for three days. Soon he would slip into a coma, with death only hours away. Left alone deliberately to slowly perish of unmitigated hunger.

All he wanted was his mother.

Epilogue

William's body will never be discovered.

He had been dead for three days when Faith finally removed his decaying corpse from the fly-infested stone tomb. She'd happily left him there as she did what she loved to do; research. Hours had been spent reading up on her chosen subject, 'Can pigs eat a human?'

She was pleased to discover that indeed they could if you had enough of them.

The article was extremely helpful. You need about sixteen pigs to eat a body weighing roughly 200 pounds, which was about 14 stones. In the end, William must have weighed no more than 126 pounds, which was about 9 stones. Farmer Childs had fifteen pigs on her land.

Perfect.

With the help of Agatha, that's what she did. She fed Farmer Childs' pigs for him, as she said she would, that weekend when he rang to say he was poorly and would she mind looking after them for a couple of days. She didn't lie when she told him that it would be a pleasure.

It had given her great satisfaction to watch the pigs devour the Grey Trench Coat Man, including his bones. Faith would never be anyone's victim.

The police never did come knocking at Faith's door and the media stories regarding William's disappearance have stopped. PC Moore is now selling drugs illegally for his new girlfriend, Katherine Parkhurst. In six months, he will be arrested and later charged with the offence and sentenced to twelve months in prison.

DCI Webb's years on the force told him that something wasn't quite right with the case dubbed the Grey Trench Coat Man. He didn't believe that William Channing had disappeared. He thought he had either taken his own life or been murdered. Frustrated, he was forced to step back when the investigation didn't turn up any new information.

What he didn't know was that, with the support of DC Earle and DC Sterling, in only a few short years, he will be investigating another murder. This time, the suspect will leave behind DNA to link them to the missing William Channing.

Dorothy Heist passed away only months before her sister Elizabeth Channing, from pneumonia. She died knowing she had got away with murdering her unfaithful husband. Natalie Winter is the only remaining sibling, she battles daily with her alcohol addiction and liver disease.

Faith decided to stay in England and start living her life, rather than existing. She rescued a two-year-old Golden Labrador and named him Guzzle, aptly named after William's encounter with fifteen pigs. Her new 'From My Kitchen' online business is growing each month. Going back to her skills of living in France, she has decided to make jam and sell it, with various country flavours from rose petal, plum and vanilla to blueberry and apple.

Agatha remained very quiet for weeks after William's death. Faith presumed that her daughter was still angry with her. She wasn't. She loved her maman and had forgiven her for her moment of weakness when she had given William some water and thought he was worthy of life.

Agatha was battling with her own dark thoughts. She liked the power she had felt when her father was dying in the outhouse. She liked the feeling when she had lured him from the café knowing, that moments later, he would be drugged in the back of her maman's car.

When she watched the pigs eat him in about nine minutes, she thought about how easy it was to commit and get away with murder.

The apple hadn't fallen far from the tree.

Acknowledgements

Well, where do I start? I have wanted to write since a young child. Life, a full-time job, and two children meant my focus has been elsewhere. In 1997, I created the characters Faith Taylor, William, and Elizabeth Channing. I wrote little but not very often over the years, and carried the story around in my head until January 2023 when I finally finished a first draft.

A huge thank you to Sunday Times best-selling author, Michael Heppell and author of Write that Book. I wouldn't have finally got my book over the line without Michael's motivation, vast knowledge, and the other Write That Book budding authors.

To proofreader and editor, Christine Beech thank you! If it hadn't been for Christine's eye of a hawk and memory like an elephant, some of the characters' ages would have been incorrect (by about six years!) and the reader would have had a noun instead of an adjective! I'll not mention all my typos!

Thank you to the author of Jackfruit Treasure Trap, Matthew Bird, for typesetting, polishing up the design, and getting Coming for You publish-ready. I've learned so much from you – mainly the process is much more technical than I thought!

My brother Martin, thank you for always being supportive when I said I wanted to be an author. You can always rely on me to send you sarcastic birthday cards and funny presents. You're welcome!

To my children Dan and Megan, never give up on achieving your dreams.

Sadly my Nan is no longer with us, I think of, and miss her every single day. Her words of wisdom and views, appear in this book and gave me the idea for the second one.

Everyone needs a Pauline in their life! Always there if I need you, thanks for all the coaching! And to Lynder, losing my job after 33 years was tough to get my head around. Thank you for the coffee and special gift. You've no idea how much your words helped.

I want to especially thank Simon, for all his belief, understanding, and constant support. I should spend the weekend writing more often, you make the best roast dinner! I couldn't ask for a better partner to take a huge leap of faith, into the unknown with.

And finally, to anyone who had bought, recommended, or read this book. You get the biggest thank you of all!

About the Author

Frances Mackintosh was born and lives in Sunderland with her daughter and partner, Simon. She worked in local government for thirty-three years, in a role that involved understanding, predicting, and interpreting behaviour, before leaving and writing Coming for You, her debut novel.

She studied Psychology and Criminology at Sunderland University and has used her expertise and passion for personality profiling to create the psychotic Grey Trench Coat Man.

To get in touch please email:
francesmackintosh.author@gmail.com